STAR WARS

EPISODE I

THE VISUAL DICTIONARY

Sensor implant

Long fingers to
draw blood

Tracker utility vest

Short-range pistol

Protective
body paint

Long-range
projectile rifle

Heavy leather
boots for
desert travel

AURRA SING

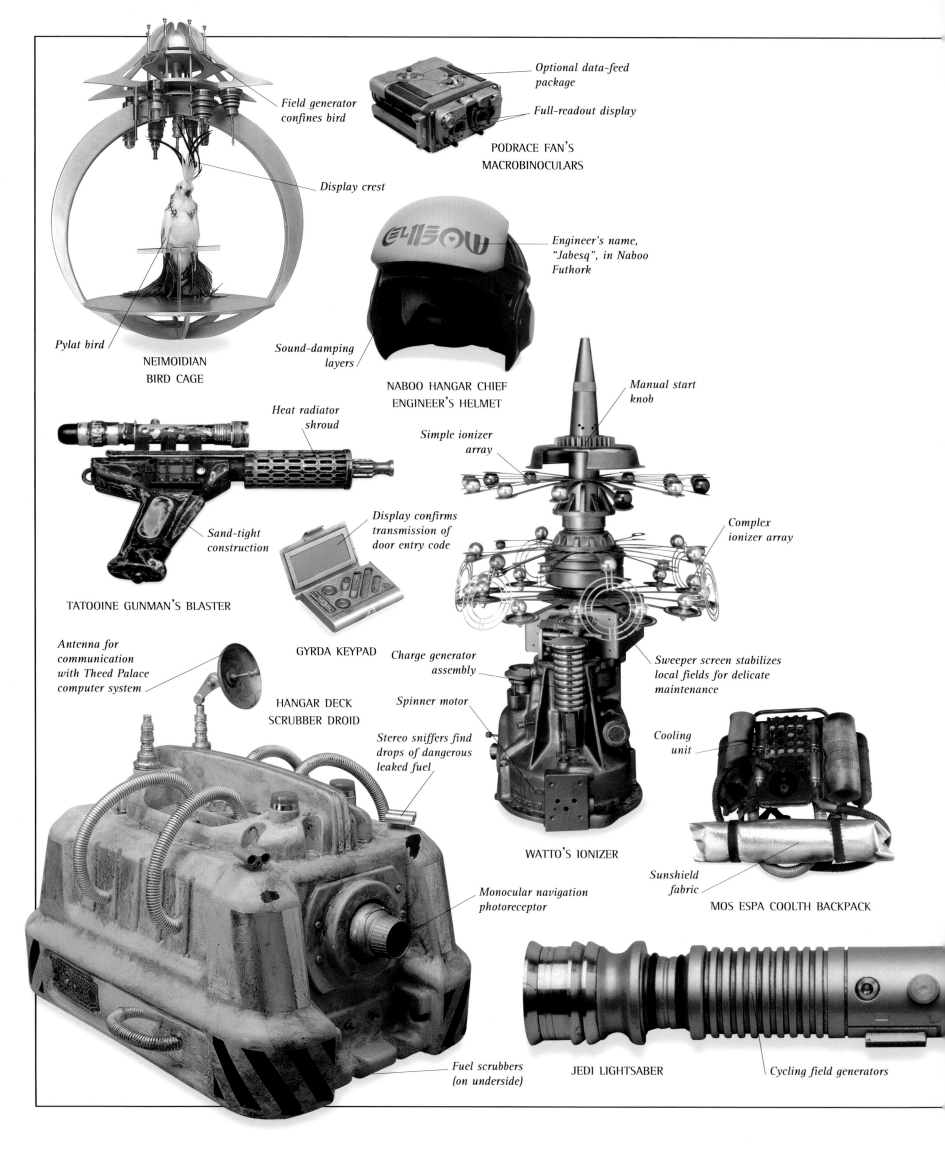

Field generator
confines bird

Optional data-feed
package

Full-readout display

PODRACE FAN'S
MACROBINOCULARS

Display crest

Pylat bird

NEIMOIDIAN
BIRD CAGE

Engineer's name,
"Jabesq", in Naboo
Futhork

Sound-damping
layers

NABOO HANGAR CHIEF
ENGINEER'S HELMET

Heat radiator
shroud

Manual start
knob

Simple ionizer
array

TATOOINE GUNMAN'S BLASTER

Sand-tight
construction

Display confirms
transmission of
door entry code

Complex
ionizer array

GYRDA KEYPAD

Charge generator
assembly

Sweeper screen stabilizes
local fields for delicate
maintenance

Antenna for
communication
with Theed Palace
computer system

HANGAR DECK
SCRUBBER DROID

Spinner motor

Stereo sniffers find
drops of dangerous
leaked fuel

Cooling
unit

WATTO'S IONIZER

Monocular navigation
photoreceptor

Sunshield
fabric

MOS ESPA COOLTH BACKPACK

JEDI LIGHTSABER

Cycling field generators

Fuel scrubbers
(on underside)

Single antenna

COMLINK

BLISSL TUNER
(MUSICAL INSTRUMENT)

STAR WARS®

EPISODE I

THE VISUAL DICTIONARY

Written by
DAVID WEST REYNOLDS

Fuel lines

Afterburner

Lubricant hose

Absurdly heavy load

Pit droid near collapse

Lead pit droid

PIT DROIDS CARRYING PODRACER ENGINE

LUCAS BOOKS

DK

DK PUBLISHING, INC.

Emitter assembly

SLAVE QUARTERS BRAZIER

Contents

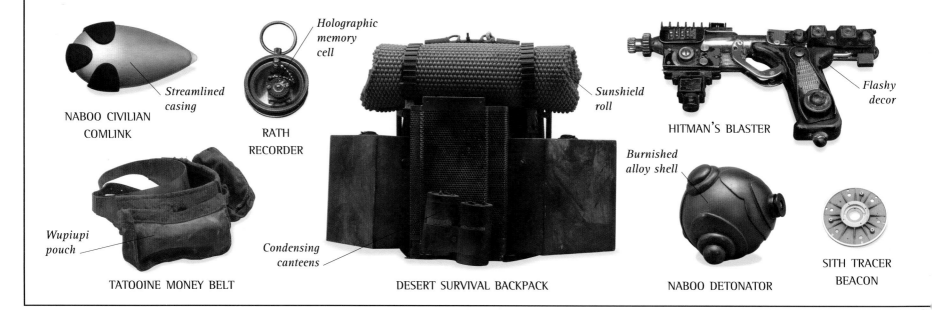

NABOO CIVILIAN COMLINK
Streamlined casing

RATH RECORDER
Holographic memory cell

Wupiupi pouch

TATOOINE MONEY BELT

DESERT SURVIVAL BACKPACK
Sunshield roll
Condensing canteens

HITMAN'S BLASTER
Flashy decor

NABOO DETONATOR
Burnished alloy shell

SITH TRACER BEACON

Introduction

EPISODE I travels back to the beginning of the *Star Wars* saga, a generation before Luke Skywalker meets Ben Kenobi and sets out on his path to destiny. In this era, Luke Skywalker's father Anakin is nine years old, and the great free Galactic Republic still stands, although its power is starting to falter. This time is populated with new characters, whose worlds are replete with gleaming spacecraft, intricate clothing, and exotic-looking robots. Just as in the real world, these artifacts tell a story. They are clues to identity. From the deathly pale appearance of Trade Federation battle droids to the tasty gorgs of Mos Espa marketplace and the fangs of the colo claw fish, the Visual Dictionary is your guide to the dazzling worlds explored in this new episode of the *Star Wars* fantasy. Because even at the beginning, there's a lot to catch up on. So jump on board.

And brace yourself.

NABOO ROYAL
STARSHIP

Hooded cloak

Hidden visage

Sith clasp

The Phantom Menace

FOUNDED LONG AGO, the Republic has united countless thousands of star systems under a single, far-reaching government. In millennia past, great sections of the Republic fought each other even as they clung to threads of unity. Peace and justice came to prevail under the protection of the wise and powerful Jedi, who draw on a mystical power known as the Force. Through the guidance of the Galactic Senate, civilization grew and the Republic became prosperous. But the price of comfort was weakness. The institutions of government became decadent and Jedi numbers dwindled to a mere ten thousand. Now, the Force itself is unbalanced and great change seems imminent...

Coruscant

A world enveloped in a single city, Coruscant is the home of galactic government and the effective center of the known universe. Representatives from

all member worlds congregate here to participate in the colossal enterprise of galactic government. From among the thousands within the senate chamber, the pleas of a single voice must be heard to save the small planet of Naboo from invasion.

On Coruscant, the leadership of the Galactic Senate is served by the Jedi—guardians of peace and justice in the Galaxy. It is on the decisions and actions of the Jedi High Council that the fate of the galaxy will turn as the forces of darkness begin to gather their strength.

Darth Sidious

The Sith Lord Darth Sidious sets into motion the final stages of his order's 2,000-year-old plan to destroy the Jedi. Working patiently, Sidious has extended his power and influence deep into the galactic government. Using his grasp of psychology and bureaucracy to stifle justice, he brings about the crisis he needs to make his move for domination.

Coruscant provides a hiding place for the mysterious Sith. This ancient dark order has been waiting in the shadows, preparing to prey upon the Galactic Republic's time of weakness and usher in a new era of Sith rule. This phantom menace radiates outward from the center, drawing into its web individuals and worlds that lie far beyond Coruscant.

Naboo

Theed Royal Palace *Palace forecourt* *Naboo philosophers*

The provincial and little-populated planet of Naboo has benefited greatly from membership in the Republic. Within an idyll of serenity, Naboo decorative architecture expresses the planet's philosophy of arts and a harmonious way of life. The Naboo have come to regard their privilege as a birthright, and do not realize the extent to which they are dependent on the core strength of galactic government to protect them. Only when crisis descends will they face the frightening realization that the only strength they can depend on is their own.

Expressive of Naboo style in its glistening silver finish and dreamlike, artful contours, the Royal Starship is nonetheless built around a core of foreign-made engine systems. Naboo society is similarly dependent on outside industry.

Hydrostatic bubbles keep out water

Overload burnout scar *Area of field leakage* *Naboo-made charge planes* *Gungan-style artistic floor pattern*

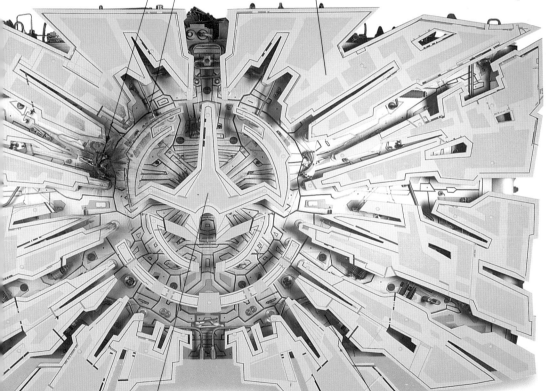

Otoh Gunga

Removed from outside contact, the underwater Gungan cities of Naboo glisten like scintillating jewelry. The Gungan capital city, Otoh Gunga, prides itself on being independent of foreign influences. Nonetheless, it relies upon a quiet but vital trade with the Naboo. In this, as in the danger they face from the Trade Federation, the Gungans find that they are more connected with outsiders than they confess.

Typical Gungan design

Core chamber holds Nubian T-14 generator *Hyperdrive effect channels improve supralight performance*

Hyperdrive Core

A dazzling example of Naboo style, the hyperdrive core of the Royal Starship is an intricate maze of charge planes and effect channels that allows the ship to slip smoothly beyond lightspeed. When the Nubian-made hyperdrive generator inside the core fails under the energy overloads encountered in battle, the Naboo begin to learn the realities of their dependence on the outside world.

TOUCHDOWN ON TATOOINE
The Naboo Royal Starship is forced by the broken hyperdrive core to land on the desert world of Tatooine. Queen Amidala must seek refuge in this wilderness and stake her hopes on desperate chance.

Slave quarters *Rough adobe walls*

Tatooine

Beyond the reach of the Republic are the worlds of the Outer Rim, a frontier where extremes of freedom and slavery coexist. Tatooine is ruled by wealthy trading barons and gangsters. The adobe architecture of Mos Espa looks as rugged and primitive as the planet itself, but the thick walls hide sophisticated interior cooling systems. On Tatooine, not everything is what it seems—as those aboard the Naboo Royal Starship find when they encounter a slave boy named Anakin Skywalker.

Mace Windu

SENIOR MEMBER of the Jedi Council, Mace Windu's wisdom and self-sacrifice is legendary. In a long and adventurous career, he has repeatedly risked his life to resolve great conflicts in fairness to both sides. Windu is sober and cool-minded but is also capable of dramatic actions in the face of danger. Even experienced Jedi look to this great man in times of serious trouble. Always ready to risk himself, Mace Windu is very reluctant to risk the lives of others. In particular, he is wary of fellow Jedi Qui-Gon Jinn's headstrong belief in Anakin Skywalker, and senses great danger with the boy. These concerns weigh heavily upon him as he considers them against his friendship and respect for Qui-Gon.

Time and again, Mace Windu has stood at the center of great conflicts. His fame has only added to his negotiating skills.

Under-tunic

Tunic

Jedi robe

Utility belt

Lightsaber

Deflector shield generator

Docking ring

Crew lounge

Color indicates diplomatic status

Cockpit

Diplomatic salon pod

Republic Cruiser

Jedi, diplomats, and ambassadors travel to trouble spots around the galaxy aboard the Republic Cruiser. This vessel's striking red color declares its political neutrality. In its well-armored salon pods, high-level negotiations take place between factions in conflict.

The Jedi High Council is secretly called upon by Supreme Chancellor Valorum of the Galactic Senate to settle the conflict with the Trade Federation. Mace Windu summons a pair of his most able Jedi for the mission. Windu little suspects the evil and danger awaiting Jedi Master Qui-Gon Jinn and his apprentice Obi-Wan Kenobi within the Trade Federation fleet.

Blade projection plate

Blade modulation circuitry

Handgrip ridges

Activator

Blade length adjust

Radiator casing segment

MACE WINDU'S LIGHTSABER

DATA FILE

◆ The Jedi use the lightsaber as a symbol of their dedication to combat in defense, not attack, and of their philosophical concern for finely tuned mind and body skills.

◆ Ambassadors, mediators, and counselors, Jedi are warriors only as a last resort.

Yoda

WELL INTO HIS 800s, Yoda is the oldest member of the Jedi High Council, as well as its most deeply perceptive Master. A great traveler in his younger years, Yoda has quietly visited hundreds of worlds on his own, spending years learning different lifeways and appreciating the infinitely variable nuances of the Force. His experiences have made him cautious and reflective. Yoda takes a personal interest in the progress of Qui-Gon Jinn and his apprentice Obi-Wan Kenobi. Yoda recognizes their considerable strength and potential even as he disagrees with some of their "dangerously reckless" choices.

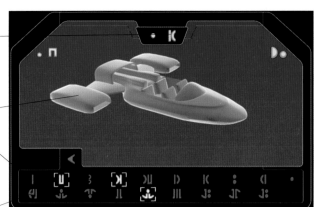

Test series indicator

Hidden image tests extrasensory perception

Test sequence

Ability testing sequence

Testing Screen

The Jedi High Council use multi-function viewscreens to test Jedi apprentices. These screens are built without buttons and are operated by Jedi mind powers. Only Force-attuned individuals can follow the high-speed series of images generated on screen. Testing screens keep the Jedi Council members in constant practice with their Force abilities.

The Jedi draw their power from the Force, an omnipresent, subtle energy field surrounding all living things. The Force can lend telekinetic powers and give insights into the future, the past, or the thoughts of others.

Tension band indicator

Testing screen displays transmitted or recorded information

Control probe

Standard tests stored in memory cell

Handgrip

Power cell

Memory cap

Test results are recorded in removable memory cell

Sensitive ears

Blade emitter shroud

Activator matrix

YODA'S LIGHTSABER

REVERSE VIEW

Custom-made Council seat

Having seen so much of life, Yoda views all that happens with a long perspective. Less active now than in his younger years, Yoda remains one of the two most important voices of wisdom on the Jedi High Council along with Mace Windu.

Well-worn Jedi robe

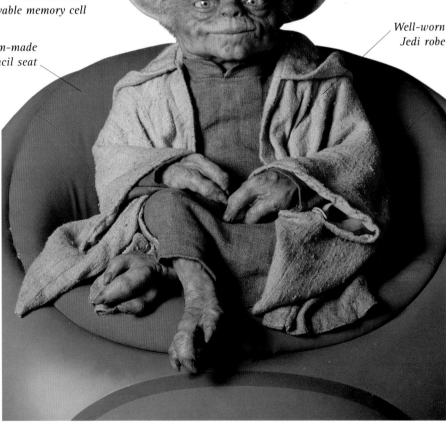

DATA FILE

◆ Yoda's gimer stick cane helps him to walk long distances and contains natural plant substances that aid meditation when chewed.

◆ It has been many years since Yoda has needed to wield his special lightsaber. Yoda takes quiet satisfaction in finding nonviolent solutions.

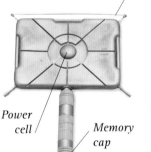

The Jedi High Council

THE TWELVE MEMBERS of the Jedi High Council represent a gathering of great minds who have proven themselves and their abilities in the service of peace and justice. Confident in their attunement to the Force, the Council members work together in trust, free from the petty constraints of ego and jealousy. Their Council Chamber is a place of open thought and speech, a realm of mutual respect and a haven of shared noble purpose. The Council is composed of five permanent members who have accepted a lifetime commitment to the difficult work of the Jedi. In addition, four long-term members serve until they choose to step down and three limited-term members sit for specified terms. This balance of membership keeps the Council wise and vigorous.

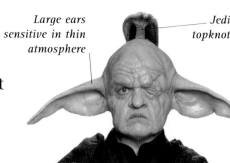

Large ears sensitive in thin atmosphere

Jedi topknot

EVEN PIELL
Jedi Master Even Piell bears a scar across his eye as a grisly trophy of a victory against terrorists who made the mistake of underestimating the diminutive Jedi Master.

The Council Chamber is located atop the central spire of the Jedi Temple on the galactic capital planet, Coruscant. The 12 members sit in a ring of chairs that are spaced equally around the chamber.

Yarael Poof

The attenuated Quermian Yarael Poof is the consummate master of Jedi mind tricks. He uses Force suggestions to bring conflicts to an abrupt end, turning combatants' own fears against themselves.

Quermian upper brain

Quermians are noseless as they smell with olfactory organs in their hands

Long neck for peering above low vegetation mats

Robe hides second set of arms and chest with lower brain

Traditional Quermian cannom collar

Tough skin impervious to high winds of Iktotchon

Well-developed horns

Customary humanoid Jedi robes

Saesee Tiin

An Iktotchi pilot, Saesee Tiin is best able to focus while traveling at extremely high speeds—at the controls of the finest spacecraft. He offers a unique perspective on the Council as his telepathic mind is always racing ahead to foresee possibilities.

Large brain supported by second heart

Surcoat adapted from ancient Cerean garb

Lightsaber

Cerean cuffs

Plain trousers

Ki-Adi-Mundi

A Jedi Knight from the largely unspoiled paradise world of Cerea, Ki-Adi-Mundi's high-domed head holds a complex binary brain. Recently added to the Council, Ki-Adi-Mundi has not yet taken a Padawan learner.

EETH KOTH

Vestigial horn patterns identify races of Iridonian Zabrak

Tholoth headdress

Iridonian Zabrak such as Eeth Koth are renowned for their mental discipline, which allows them to tolerate great physical suffering. This ability is born of surviving their harsh homeworld.

Dense hair deters biting cygnats of Thisspias

Adi Gallia

Born into a highly placed diplomatic family stationed on Coruscant, the intuitive Adi Gallia often seems to know what people are about to say. Gallia has many contacts throughout the Coruscant political machine, making her one of the Supreme Chancellor's most valuable intelligence sources.

Protective goggles

Antiox mask

Highly developed extrasensory organs

PLO KOON
A Kel Dor from Dorin, Plo Koon must protect his sensitive eyes and nostrils from the oxygen-rich atmosphere of Coruscant with special devices.

Jedi robe

Gallia's second lightsaber replaces her first, which was destroyed on a mission

Utility pouch

OPPO RANCISIS
Abdicating his throne on Thisspias, Oppo Rancisis instead sought to serve the entire galaxy among the Jedi order based on Coruscant. When negotiations fail, Rancisis ensures that Jedi-counseled military tactics are cunning and effective.

Mark of illumination

Tall travel boots

DEPA BILLABA
Adopting the traditional culture of Chalacta to honor her slain parents, Depa Billaba offers an ordered perspective to the wide-ranging minds of the Council.

Youthful topknot

Yaddle

Young at only 477, Jedi Master Yaddle looks up to Yoda while leading the Council with compassion and balanced patience. Yaddle silently waits in discussions before offering her single, powerful, soft-spoken comment.

DATA FILE

◆ The 12 High Council members reflect a mere hint of the diversity within the Jedi ranks, which include members of hundreds of species and cultures.

◆ Of the teeming trillions of species that populate the galaxy, very few individuals become full-fledged Jedi Knights: the ranks based on Coruscant number only about 10,000.

Qui-Gon Jinn
JEDI MASTER

MASTER QUI-GON JINN is an experienced Jedi who has proven his value to the leadership of the Jedi order in many important missions and difficult negotiations. In his maturity, however, he remains as restless as he was in his youth. When Qui-Gon encounters young Anakin Skywalker on the Outer Rim desert world of Tatooine, the Jedi is deeply struck by an unshakeable sense that the boy is part of the galaxy's destiny. In boldly championing the cause of Anakin, Qui-Gon sets in motion momentous events that will ultimately bring balance to the Force—but not without great cost.

Long hair worn back to keep vision clear

Jedi robe

On the desert planet of Tatooine, Qui-Gon wishes to avoid being recognized as a Jedi. Accordingly, he trades his customary Jedi robe for a rough-spun poncho such as those worn by local settlers and moisture farmers.

REPUBLIC CRUISER
Dispatched by the Supreme Chancellor of the Galactic Senate to settle the Trade Federation dispute, Qui-Gon travels on board the diplomatic vessel *Radiant VII*.

Jedi tunic

Orientation grids

As the *Radiant VII* prepares to land within the Trade Federation flagship's hangar, navigation readouts ensure precise maneuvers.

Neimoidian flagship

DESTINATION NAVISPHERE

Mode indicator

Trajectory path shows route ahead

Radiant VII

Lightsaber

Following the custom of his day, Qui-Gon has built a lightsaber with a highly elaborate internal design. Multiple small power cells are stored in the scalloped handgrip and microscopic circuitry governs the nature of the energy blade. Simpler lightsaber designs, built outside the halls of the Jedi Temple on Coruscant, typically use a single large power cell inside a solid handgrip.

Blade projection plate

Activator

Series of micro-cells

Charging port

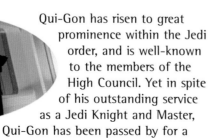

Qui-Gon has risen to great prominence within the Jedi order, and is well-known to the members of the High Council. Yet in spite of his outstanding service as a Jedi Knight and Master, Qui-Gon has been passed by for a seat on the Council. This is due to his bold, headstrong nature and his favoring of risk and action, which sometimes bring him into disagreement with his Jedi peers and elders.

QUI-GON JINN'S LIGHTSABER

Rugged travel boots

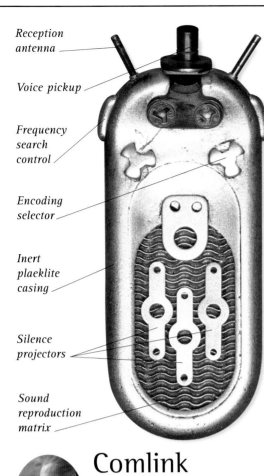

Reception antenna

Voice pickup

Frequency search control

Encoding selector

Inert plaeklite casing

Silence projectors

Sound reproduction matrix

Holoprojector

One of the utility devices that Qui-Gon carries is a small holoprojector. This can be tuned with a comlink to carry a hologram transmission for face-to-face contact, or it can be used as an independent image recorder and projector.

Qui-Gon loads his holoprojector with selected images from the technical databanks onboard the Naboo Royal Starship. He intends to use them to help obtain repair parts when the ship is grounded on Tatooine.

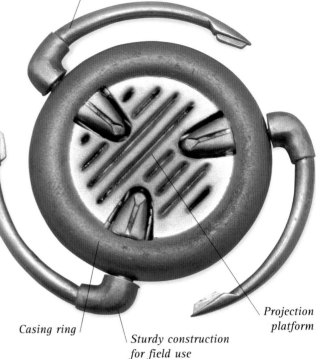

Tines rotate downward to plug into signal feed or to link to larger image projector

Projection platform

Casing ring

Sturdy construction for field use

TOYDARIAN TROUBLE

Some species are naturally immune to the "Jedi mind tricks" of all but the most powerful Masters. Qui-Gon Jinn has never even heard of a Toydarian before he encounters Watto on Tatooine and the Jedi soon finds that he needs more than Force-assisted "suggestions" to persuade the hovering junk dealer to cooperate with him.

Comlink

Qui-Gon's miniature comlink allows him to keep in touch with Obi-Wan Kenobi when the two operate separately. It features complex security devices to prevent unauthorized interception and is unlabeled to thwart use by non-Jedi. A silence projector lends privacy to conversations and helps Qui-Gon maintain stealth in the field.

COMLINK
REVERSE VIEW

On meeting Anakin, Qui-Gon believes he has recognized the prophesied individual who will restore balance and harmony to the Force. The Jedi feels so strongly that he has recognized this individual that he is not persuaded otherwise by members of the Jedi High Council, including the influential Yoda, who sense danger in the boy.

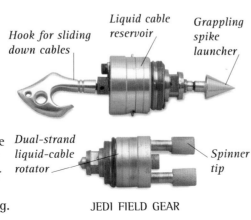

Qui-Gon earned the rank of Master when he trained his first Padawan apprentice to Knighthood, although his second apprentice failed to become a Knight. Obi-Wan is Qui-Gon's third Padawan and a worthy student of his wisdom and skill.

On Tatooine, Qui-Gon battles a Sith warrior wielding a deadly lightsaber. Since lightsabers are seldom handled by non-Jedi, the order primarily uses them as defense against blaster bolts rather than other lightsabers. However, lightsaber dueling is taught as part of classical Jedi training.

Hook for sliding down cables

Liquid cable reservoir

Grappling spike launcher

Dual-strand liquid-cable rotator

Spinner tip

JEDI FIELD GEAR

DATA FILE

◆ The Jedi workshops on Coruscant supply exquisite materials and tools for initiates constructing their own lightsabers. The initiates' ability to do this successfully proves their developed sensitivity to the Force.

◆ Greed and political scheming are weakening the Galactic Republic that Qui-Gon serves. In an attempt to restore lasting peace and security to the galaxy, Qui-Gon is motivated to take a more active role than that traditionally taken by the Jedi.

Obi-Wan Kenobi
JEDI KNIGHT

OBI-WAN KENOBI has followed a responsible path on his journey toward Jedi knighthood as the Padawan apprentice to Jedi Master Qui-Gon Jinn. Strongly influenced by other leading Jedi as well as by Qui-Gon, Obi-Wan is more brooding and cautious than his teacher. He is careful to weigh the consequences of his actions and is reluctant to entangle himself unnecessarily in transgressions against the will of the Jedi High Council. A serious, quiet man possessed of a dry sense of humor, Obi-Wan strives to be worthy of his order and feels honored to be Qui-Gon's student, although he worries about his Master's tendency to take risks in defiance of the Council. Nevertheless, Obi-Wan follows Qui-Gon Jinn's example and develops an independent spirit of his own.

Short hair of a Padawan apprentice

Apprentice's long braid

Tunic

Hooded robe

Utility belt

UTILITY BELT *Belt fastener* *Fastener band*

Traditional leather *Food and tool pouches*

UTILITY POUCHES
On field missions, Jedi carry a basic kit consisting of food capsules, medical supplies, multitools, and other essential devices.

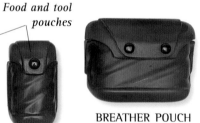

BREATHER POUCH

FOOD AND ENERGY CAPSULES

Jedi Gear

The basic Jedi clothing of belted tunic, travel boots, and robe speaks of the simplicity vested in Jedi philosophy and carries overtones of their mission as travelers. Individual Jedi keep utility belt field gear to a minimum. As initiates are taught in the great Temple, Jedi reputations are based on their spirits and not on material trappings.

A99 Aquata Breather

In this era, Jedi Knights usually carry various high-tech devices concealed in their robes or in belt pouches. On their mission to Naboo, Obi-Wan and Qui-Gon Jinn carry A99 Aquata breathers, knowing that much of the planet's surface is water. Breathers allow the Jedi to survive underwater for up to two hours. In other times, Jedi have avoided such technological devices in order to minimize their dependence on anything but their own resourcefulness.

Rugged travel boots

Regulator

Hinges for storage

Mouthpiece

Compressed air tanks

Blade
modulation
circuitry

Blade emitter

Blade length
and intensity
control

Activator

Internal
blade
crystals

Single main
internal
power cell

Handgrip

Charging
port

Power
cell
reserve
cap

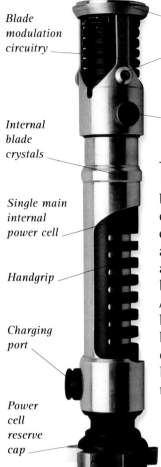

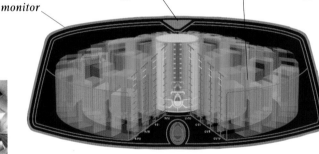

Faced with the mechanized minions of the Trade Federation droid army, Obi-Wan knows that he need not exercise the combat restraint he would use with living beings. He puts his fight training to good use, yet maintains cool concentration.

Voice pickup

Encoder

Silencer

OBI-WAN
KENOBI'S
COMLINK

Centered
awareness

Battle
stance

Lightsaber

Lightsabers follow a common design. Optional elements, like blade power and length modulators, are small and unobtrusive. Accordingly, Jedi lightsabers appear similar at first glance. A closer inspection, however, reveals that lightsabers rarely look exactly alike. All are hand-built by the initiates themselves, making design details a matter of individual choice. Most Padawan apprentices build their lightsabers to resemble those of their teachers as a mark of respect.

Hyperdrive
diagnostic
monitor

Warning mark indicates
energy leak

Damaged priming
pylons

Blue
lightsaber
blade

Obi-Wan Kenobi views Anakin Skywalker as an unnecessary risk, both as a travel companion and as a potential Jedi. But at Qui-Gon Jinn's request, Obi-Wan accepts Anakin as his apprentice, beginning a long and fateful relationship.

Hyperdrive

When the hyperdrive generator of the Naboo Royal Starship is damaged, Obi-Wan stays on board to look after the drive core while Qui-Gon seeks a replacement generator. Constantly monitoring the damaged component, Obi-Wan readies the core for repairs.

Obi-Wan is an exceptional lightsaber duelist and a formidable opponent for Darth Maul. The Sith Lord fights with inhuman intensity, fueled by the hateful energy of the dark side of the Force. In the heat of mortal combat and on the brink of death, Obi-Wan faces the temptation to draw on the same terrible strength in order to defeat his enemy.

DATA FILE

◆ Jedi robes are virtually indistinguishable from the simple robes worn by many species throughout the galaxy. This signifies the Jedi pledge to the service and protection of even the most humble galactic citizen.

◆ Obi-Wan remains loyal to Qui-Gon even when this puts him at odds with the Jedi High Council.

The Neimoidians

RAISED AS GRUBS until the age of seven, young Neimoidians are kept in communal hives and given limited amounts of food. The less acquisitive ones are allowed to die as others hoard more than they can eat. This practice makes Neimoidians greedy and fearful of death. As adults, Neimoidians are known for their exceptional organizing abilities. Driven by their intense desire for possessions, they have built the largest commercial corporation in the galaxy. Led by Neimoidians, the Trade Federation is a labyrinthine organization of bureaucrats and trade officials from many worlds that has insinuated itself throughout the galaxy.

Diplomatic ploov

Neimoidian senatorial miter

Ferrous pigmented sclera

Supreme representative mantle

Financial officer's collar

Diplomatic ploov

NEIMOIDIAN DRESS
In status-obsessed Neimoidian society, elaborate clothing asserts the wearer's wealth and social position over other jealous Neimoidians. Hats, cloaks, and drapes, as well as colors and fabrics, all have particular symbolic meanings.

THE BLOCKADE OF NABOO
The shadowy figure of Darth Sidious has incited key individuals within the Neimoidian Inner Circle to take drastic measures in pursuit of profit. When the Galactic Senate imposes taxation on the former Free Trade Zones of the outlying systems, Sidious goads the Trade Federation into aggressively blockading the planet of Naboo in retaliation—a measure by which he intends to force an end to the new regulations.

Antenna receives summons signal from Sith Lord

Micro-screen

DARTH SIDIOUS' SUMMONING CHIPS

Insincere gesture of innocence

Heavy deflector-shield gear

Cockpit is sealed since shuttle is piloted entirely by instruments

Landing gear flexure equipment

Lounge in center

Degreasing compound mister

Antiseptic gas nozzle

Generator vents

SHUTTLE AIRLOCK STERILIZING MODULE

Insanely expensive Tyrian violet cloth

Pointed claws imitate those of living beetles

Boarding ramp

Outer hatch (open)

Lott Dod

The Trade Federation is so powerful that it is represented in the Galactic Senate—an ominous situation. Its senator, Lott Dod, uses bureaucratic lies and procedural tricks to further Trade Federation aims from his Senate seat. Even Dod, however, was unable to thwart the new taxes that threaten to cut into Trade Federation profits.

NEIMOIDIAN SHUTTLE PASSENGER SECTION
Recalling the body shapes of giant domesticated beetles on Neimoidia, the Neimoidian shuttle conveys trade officers from orbiting freighters to planet surfaces and the hangars of other vessels. The pointed landing claws are only effective on hard surfaces, because Neimoidians are not interested in landing on bare fields.

Rune Haako

As Settlement Officer of the Trade Federation armed forces, Rune Haako serves as diplomatic attaché and legal counsel to Nute Gunray. Haako has a reputation for ruthlessly treating business partners as adversaries and conniving to wrest every last credit from them.

Neimoidians are cautious by nature and the Trade Federation has always been careful to hide its acts of extortion and manipulation behind lies and protests of good faith. Their open aggression against Naboo is new territory for them, and both Gunray and Haako are uneasy about the possibility of escalation.

Attorney's cowl

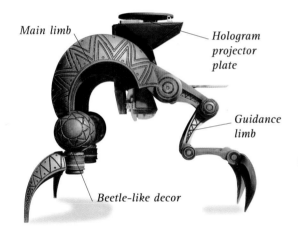

Main limb

Hologram projector plate

Guidance limb

Beetle-like decor

MECHNO-CHAIR
Walking mechno-chairs are neither comfortable nor practical. However, they are hugely expensive and express the high status of their user. They also serve as platforms for hologram transmissions of high-ranking individuals.

Nute Gunray

A Commanding Viceroy of the Trade Federation, Nute Gunray wields great authority and serves on the Trade Federation Executive Board. Deceitful and willing to kill for his far-reaching commercial aims, Gunray directs the actions of the secret army fleet from the bridge of the flagship.

Viceroy's crested tiara

Wheedling expression

Viceroy's collar

Underhanded gesture

DATA FILE

◆ The Neimoidians' organizational skills come from running mass hives and vast fungus farms on their home world of Neimoidia.

◆ Trade Federation freighters, hauling cargo between the far-flung stars of the Republic, are a familiar sight in orbit above many civilized worlds.

The Invasion Force

WHEN THE BLOCKADE fails to intimidate the Naboo Queen into submission, the Trade Federation prepares for the next step: invasion. The Sith Lord Darth Sidious persuades Neimoidian Viceroy Nute Gunray to order the deployment of an immense secret army hidden in the cargo hangars of converted trade freighters. The Naboo little suspect the magnitude of this force, and the Neimoidian leader commits the outrage in confidence that the weak politicians of the Galactic Senate will not object. In support of his evil plans, the viceroy is aided by the cowardly captain of the war fleet command vessel, Daultay Dofine, as well as droid soldiers and powerful war craft.

Data goggles allow pilot to see constant holographic data readouts

Comlink

Vessel command officer's miter

Skin mottled from self-indulgence

Daultay Dofine reports to Neimoidian Viceroy Nute Gunray.

Daultay Dofine

Captain of the Trade Federation's flagship vessel, Daultay Dofine has climbed the ladder of rank through a combination of high birth, back-stabbing, and groveling behavior toward his superiors. Nevertheless, Dofine finds the bold plans of the Sith Lord Darth Sidious too dangerous for his tastes. However, he soon learns that his tastes are entirely irrelevant.

A fleet of specially-built C-9979 craft land the Trade Federation invasion force on Naboo. These landing craft are built to hold heavy armor and legions of troops in their bodies and repulsorlift wings. Groups of three landing craft are deployed in a pattern that cuts off all the Naboo cities from each other.

Officer's drape

MTTs are dispatched to strategic positions, where they thunder along programmed routes.

DATA FILE

◆ Wargame exercises and action against bandits threatening trade routes tested all aspects of the Trade Federation army, ensuring that the force is completely invincible ... or so it seems.

◆ The wealthy, arrogant Neimoidians tend to avoid any kind of labor, preferring to use droids instead.

Droid deployment hatch

Heavy armor plating

Repulsorlift exhaust system

Although Trade Federation war craft have only been used in exercises and skirmishes before their deployment on Naboo, their minimum-cost paint is already badly chipped. This attests to the Neimoidians' dedication to cheapness even in this profitable and long-awaited enterprise.

Protocol droid TC-14 ignores the foul play brewing against the Jedi ambassadors for the Supreme Chancellor. When the Jedi visitors are hit with poison gas, TC-14 simply wants to get out of the way, apologizing even to the battle droids outside the meeting room.

Underestimating the number of blaster turrets bristling from the Trade Federation war freighters, Naboo pilot Ric Olié takes a near-collision course in his effort to escape the deadly line of fire.

TC-14

Frequent memory erasures ensure docility

Neutral humanoid form

Serving Viceroy Nute Gunray and his lieutenant Rune Haako of the Trade Federation, TC-14 acts as servant and translator during trade negotiations with foreign cultures. TC-14 is often employed to distract official guests while legal manipulation is carried out behind their backs.

Hangar arm   Centersphere   War forces carried in interior

Armor-plated hull

Restraining bolt mount

Triple quadlaser batteries

Trade Federation freighters seem harmless from a distance. Enemies are lulled into a false sense of security—until the heavy quadlaser batteries start firing.

War Freighter

To carry the forces of its army, the Trade Federation has secretly converted its commercial freighter fleet into battleships, replete with shields, blaster turrets, and military communication arrays. These disguised war freighters hide the deadly battle machines until they are right on top of their enemies—or, as the Trade Federation prefers to call them, "future customers."

SIDE VIEW

Multi-system connection wires

Walking wing in attack mode

WALK MODE

Active sensor "eye"

Subservient posture

Polished silver finish

Flight assault lasers

Reinforced knee joint

Walking limbtips

Droid Control Ship

Shinplate

Droid Starfighter

The complex, precision-engineered droid starfighters built for the Trade Federation by the Xi Char cathedral factories are variable-geometry machines. The long, wing-like claws open to reveal deadly laser cannons. On the ground, these "wings" become movable legs as the fighter shifts to walk mode for surface patrol.

Foot shell

All units of the Trade Federation droid army are controlled by the Central Control Computer onboard a modified war freighter. Without the control signal, droids shut down, making the Droid Control Ship a key target whose destruction could wipe out the entire invasion force.

Battle Droids

THE GALACTIC REPUBLIC has survived disagreements, standoffs, and even rebellion among its many member worlds, relying on the Jedi Knights to quell conflicts. In this enlightened age, few standing armies are maintained that serve anything other than ceremonial purposes, since an army could be regarded as an open threat to galactic peace. Nevertheless, as the bureaucracy of the Republic Senate indulges in endless debates and procedural bickering, the use of force has become a real threat. The wealthy Trade Federation has quietly gone far beyond any other group in assembling a massive army composed of ghostly, emotionless droid soldiers that are ready to do their masters' bidding without a touch of emotion or mercy. Their deployment upon the peaceful people of Naboo heralds the end of an age of peace and security in the galaxy.

Signal clarifier septode

Magnetic stabilizing field bar

Signal confirmation module

Speech transmission lines

Interference dissipator mat

Stored vocabulary triggered by control impulses

Vocoder

Sensory input cable

Receiver assembly casing

Signal transmission lines

Dephasing anticode sieve

Signal reception boost antenna

Specialized movement processor

Transmitter boost antenna

Code processing baffles

Signal receiver assembly

Sampled movement cycle memory

Signal boost and power augment backpack

Override signal receptor

Speech processor

General command storage

Optical sensor

Arm extension piston

High-torque motors

Battle Droid Head

The battle droid head, lacking a brain of its own, contains little more than a large and sensitive control signal receiver. Small processors collect movement and limited sensory data for transmission back to the Central Control Computer, and a vocoder enables the droid to talk.

STAP
Battle droid scouts and antipersonnel clean-up snipers are swept through the air on armed Single Trooper Aerial Platforms. The repulsolift STAP's minimal structure allows it to thread its way through dense forest that would be inaccessible to larger vehicles. The droid pilot rides exposed to enemy fire.

Command Officer

In order to streamline communication between Trade Federation officials and droid troops, certain battle droids, such as OOM-9, are designated Command Officers. Orders are conveyed to officer droids via priority channels from the Central Control Computer processors.

Droid type designation markings

Macrobinoculars

Enemy charge reading

Enemy mass reading

Stereo image rangefinder

OFFICER'S MACROBINOCULARS

OOM-9

Ⅱ ⅢⅠ ⅢⅠ ⅢⅡ ⅢⅢ Ⅱ

1 2 3 4 5 6 7 8 9

GALACTIC BASIC NUMERALS
IDENTIFY INDIVIDUAL DROIDS

Command Officer

Security droid

Pilot droid

Infantry battle droid

DROID TYPES
Battle droids are structurally identical irrespective of job function. To increase efficiency, however, droids are pre-programmed with specialized subroutines. Infantry and Command Officer droids are fitted with power backpacks to boost operational range and extend recharge intervals.

Dried cartilage-shaped shin plates

DATA FILE

◆ Their lack of independent thought processors make battle droids immune to fear, cowardice, or mercy pleas.

◆ The smooth movements of battle droids are the result of pre-digitized motion-capture data taken from live soldiers and broadcast by the Central Control Computer to each droid.

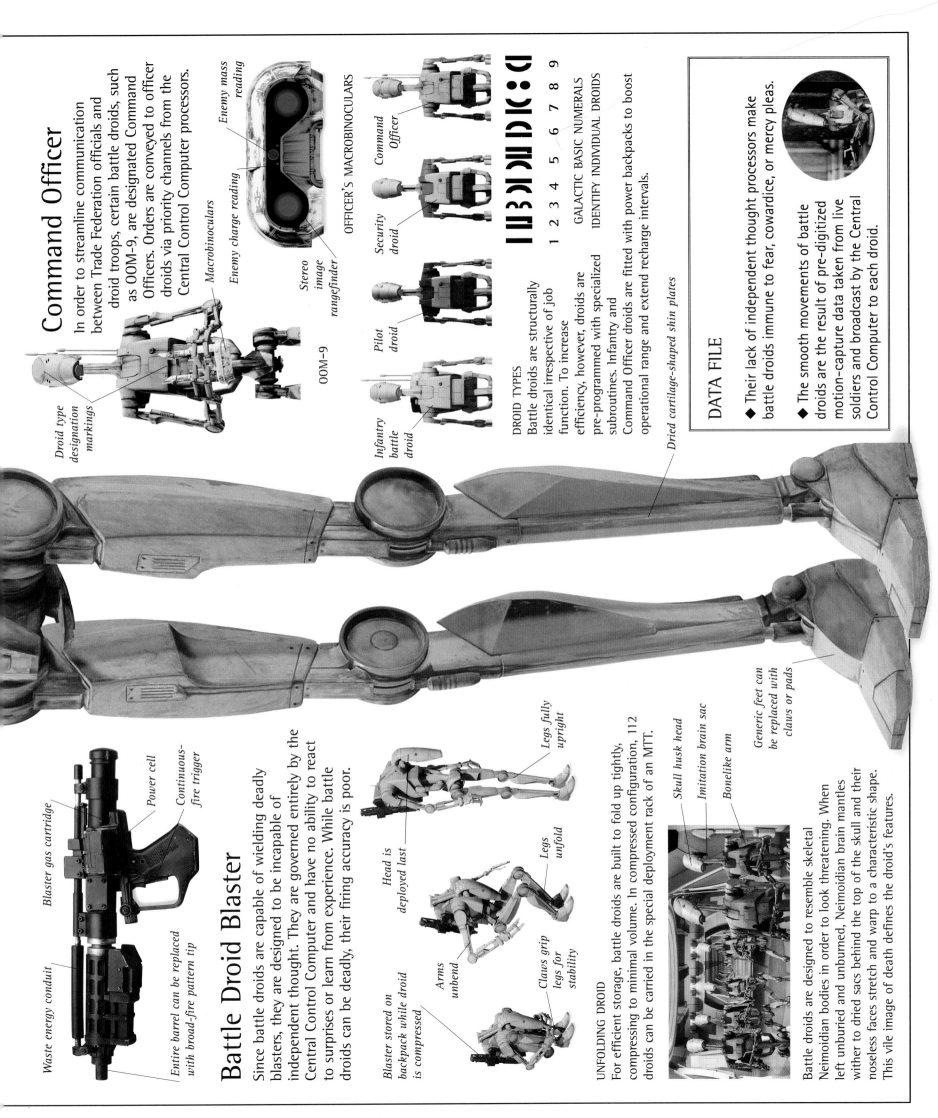

Battle Droid Blaster

Since battle droids are capable of wielding deadly blasters, they are designed to be incapable of independent thought. They are governed entirely by the Central Control Computer and have no ability to react to surprises or learn from experience. While battle droids can be deadly, their firing accuracy is poor.

Waste energy conduit

Blaster gas cartridge

Power cell

Continuous-fire trigger

Entire barrel can be replaced with broad-fire pattern tip

Head is deployed last

Legs fully upright

Legs unfold

Arms unbend

Blaster stored on backpack while droid is compressed

Claws grip legs for stability

UNFOLDING DROID
For efficient storage, battle droids are built to fold up tightly, compressing to minimal volume. In compressed configuration, 112 droids can be carried in the special deployment rack of an MTT.

Skull husk head

Imitation brain sac

Bonelike arm

Generic feet can be replaced with claws or pads

Battle droids are designed to resemble skeletal Neimoidian bodies in order to look threatening. When left unburied and unburned, Neimoidian brain mantles wither to dried sacs behind the top of the skull and their noseless faces stretch and warp to a characteristic shape. This vile image of death defines the droid's features.

Droidekas

To MAKE UP for the weaknesses of battle droids, a special contract was awarded for the creation of an altogether different combat droid that would be a much more serious weapon. The design was created by a species of chitinous Colicoids in their own image on a planet far from the Republic's core. Colicoids are known for their completely unfeeling and murderous ways, and Colla IV has been embroiled for many years in diplomatic disputes related to the death and consumption of visitors to the system. The droideka was exactly what concerned Trade Federation officers wanted: a formidable, heavy-duty killing machine to back up the battle droids in the face of determined opposition.

Triad active sensor antennas

FRONT VIEW

Head-on to an attacker, a droideka presents blazing guns and a fearsome image as well as a minimal target silhouette for opponents who survive long enough to return fire.

Using a combination of momentum and repulsor effects, droidekas unfurl in a matter of seconds from wheel form into standing position, ready to attack. The dramatic transformation recalls the attack pattern of a deadly adult Colicoid, and can take unwary opponents by surprise—as the droids' manufacturers intended.

Backshell plate protects weapons while droideka is rolling toward enemy

Lateral boom for weapon arm

Primary rolling surface

Sensor head

Sensor antenna

Sternum plate

Heavy plate upper weapon arm

Folded forward leg

Pointed claw foot

Deflector shield projector flaps

Case-hardened bronzium armor shell

Reactor cooling vanes

BACK VIEW

Desperate enemies attempting to attack a droideka from behind find that its armor is extremely effective, and its moving legs and gun arms are hard to hit.

Rear leg

Wheel Form

For compact storage and optimum travel speed, droidekas retract into the shape of a wheel. Using pulsed internal micro-repulsors in sequence, they roll themselves into battle, opening at the last minute into their combat form. In transit, the wheel configuration presents a smaller and faster target to enemy gunfire.

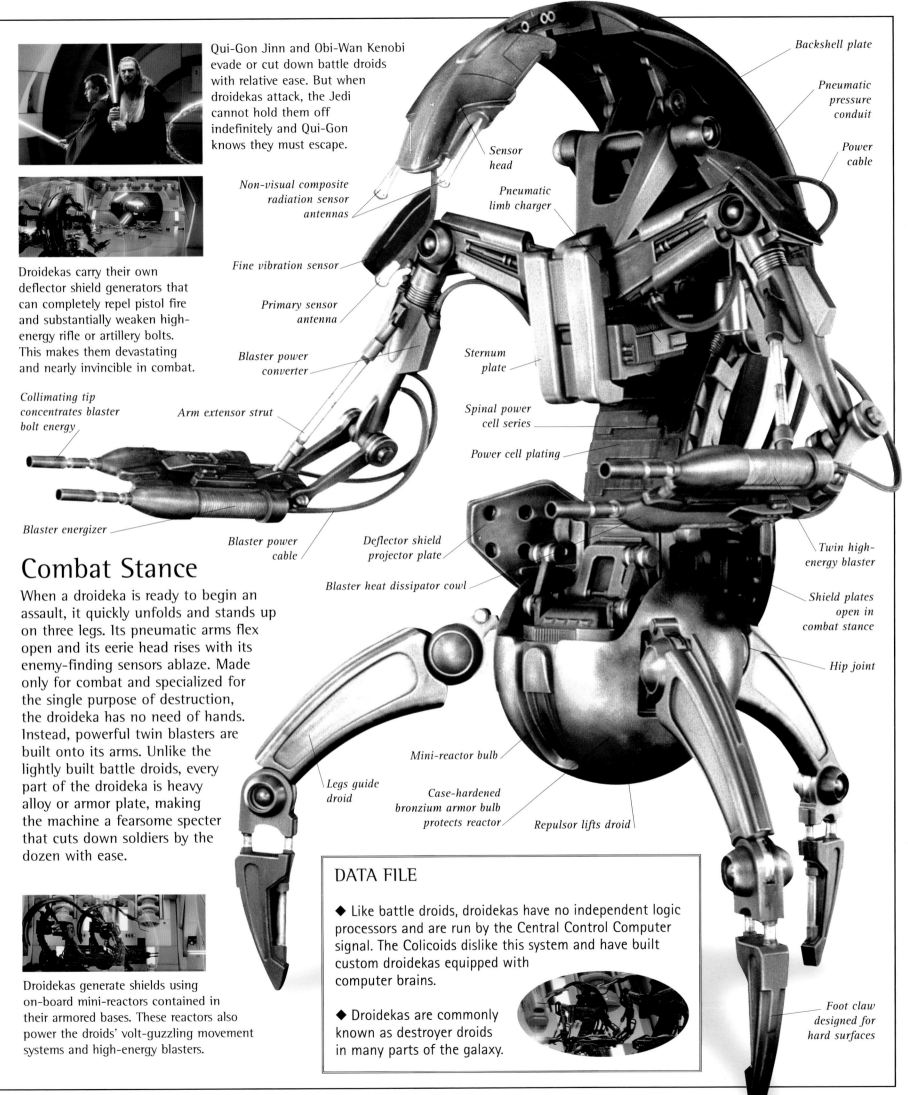

Qui-Gon Jinn and Obi-Wan Kenobi evade or cut down battle droids with relative ease. But when droidekas attack, the Jedi cannot hold them off indefinitely and Qui-Gon knows they must escape.

Droidekas carry their own deflector shield generators that can completely repel pistol fire and substantially weaken high-energy rifle or artillery bolts. This makes them devastating and nearly invincible in combat.

Collimating tip concentrates blaster bolt energy

Arm extensor strut

Blaster energizer

Blaster power cable

Combat Stance

When a droideka is ready to begin an assault, it quickly unfolds and stands up on three legs. Its pneumatic arms flex open and its eerie head rises with its enemy-finding sensors ablaze. Made only for combat and specialized for the single purpose of destruction, the droideka has no need of hands. Instead, powerful twin blasters are built onto its arms. Unlike the lightly built battle droids, every part of the droideka is heavy alloy or armor plate, making the machine a fearsome specter that cuts down soldiers by the dozen with ease.

Droidekas generate shields using on-board mini-reactors contained in their armored bases. These reactors also power the droids' volt-guzzling movement systems and high-energy blasters.

Backshell plate

Pneumatic pressure conduit

Power cable

Sensor head

Non-visual composite radiation sensor antennas

Pneumatic limb charger

Fine vibration sensor

Primary sensor antenna

Blaster power converter

Sternum plate

Spinal power cell series

Power cell plating

Deflector shield projector plate

Blaster heat dissipator cowl

Twin high-energy blaster

Shield plates open in combat stance

Hip joint

Mini-reactor bulb

Legs guide droid

Case-hardened bronzium armor bulb protects reactor

Repulsor lifts droid

Foot claw designed for hard surfaces

DATA FILE

◆ Like battle droids, droidekas have no independent logic processors and are run by the Central Control Computer signal. The Colicoids dislike this system and have built custom droidekas equipped with computer brains.

◆ Droidekas are commonly known as destroyer droids in many parts of the galaxy.

Queen Amidala

AMIDALA rules as Queen of the Naboo people at the age of only 14. She was raised by humble parents in a small mountain village, where her exceptional abilities were recognized early in life. Given the best training and pushed to develop her capabilities, she became Princess of Theed, the Naboo capital city, at the age of 12. Amidala was elected Queen upon the abdication of the previous sovereign, Veruna, who had become embroiled in outworld politics after a rule of 13 years. The Naboo trusted that Amidala would hold their interests close to her heart—but had no idea of the crisis looming ahead.

Jewel of Zenda

Gold faceframes

Hair combed over a padded form

Wide shoulders make Amidala seem larger

Hand-stitched gold embroidery

White thumbnail polish is the only tradition Amidala retains from her native village

Shed potolli fur cuffs

Illuminated sein jewel

Wide gown flare hides feet

Throne-Room Gown

Amidala draws upon Naboo's deeply traditional modes of royal dress and makeup to express the commitment she has to her role. Her extremely formal appearance in the palace throne room helps her project an unwaveringly professional image and warns others not to dismiss her abilities.

Amidala sits in state in Theed Palace, hearing cases and reports from the Advisory Council. With her clear perception, she inspires confidence even in seasoned and hard-edged men like Captain Panaka.

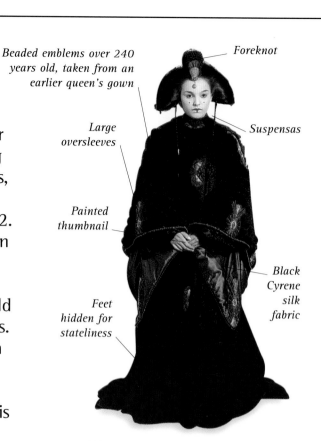

Beaded emblems over 240 years old, taken from an earlier queen's gown

Foreknot

Large oversleeves

Suspensas

Painted thumbnail

Black Cyrene silk fabric

Feet hidden for stateliness

FOREIGN RESIDENCE GOWN
On Coruscant, Amidala wears a dark gown befitting the gravity of her situation. This subdued foreign residence gown acknowledges Amidala's separation from Naboo and the peril her people face.

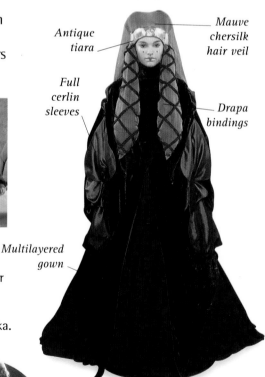

Antique tiara

Mauve chersilk hair veil

Full cerlin sleeves

Drapa bindings

Multilayered gown

AMIDALA'S TRAVELING GOWN

When Queen Amidala travels aboard the Naboo Royal Starship, she holds court in a spacious throne room. Amidala uses a holoprojector to communicate with Governor Sio Bibble back on Naboo.

GOLD BEADS

The Queen's gowns are set off with many fine details, such as beads and suspensa ornaments. Many of these come from the palace treasure rooms.

Amidala's stylized white makeup draws upon Naboo's ancient royal customs. The red "scar of remembrance" marks Naboo's time of suffering, before the Great Time of Peace.

NABOO VICTORY PARADE

Escoffiate headpiece

Royal Sovereign of Naboo medal

Golden hairbands

Scar of remembrance divides lip

Stylized beauty marks display symmetry

Royal diadem

Minimal jewelry for simplicity

Jeweled finials

Aurate fan in ancient Naboo royal fashion, signifying continuity

Suspensas made of delicate orichalc finework

Senate Gown

When Amidala pleads for her people before the Galactic Senate, she appears in an extraordinary gown and hairstyle that express the majesty of the free people of Naboo. The regal attire also hides Amidala's feelings and helps her stay courageous and aloof.

Grand finial hairtip ornaments balance escoffiate headpiece

Petaled cape

Golden, triple-braided soutache

Plain white gown expresses the pure happiness of newfound peace

Embossed rosette

Parade Gown

After the victory over the Trade Federation, Amidala appears in a parade gown markedly different from her robes of office. The silken petals of the dress resemble huge, lovely flowers found near Amidala's home village. These flowers bloom only once every 88 years, heralding a time of special celebration.

DATA FILE

◆ Naboo's monarchy is not hereditary: rulers are elected by their people on merit. Queen Amidala is not the youngest sovereign ever to rule.

◆ Amidala can step down from the throne whenever she chooses.

25

The Queen's Handmaidens

DEDICATED AND LOW-KEY, the royal handmaidens shadow Queen Amidala at all times. This select group maintains Amidala's regal image, assisting behind the scenes with her elaborate gowns, hairstyles, and makeup. They also quietly protect Amidala, acting as secret bodyguards. Upon Amidala's coronation, the handmaidens were hand picked for their intelligence, courage, fitness, and resemblance to Amidala. Although the Queen has known them for just half a year, she values their company. In particular, she has become close friends with the dependable and cool-headed Sabé.

Rabé

In spite of her young age, Rabé has learned to exercise great patience in her role as handmaiden to the Queen. She soothes Amidala's nerves and helps to prepare her exotic hairstyles, which can require several hours to perfect.

Oversleeves in the Naboo style

Soft trevella cloth

Gown tinted with spectra-fade dye

Disguised as Queen Amidala, Sabé is flanked by handmaidens in the throne room of the Royal Starship. The still, expressionless presence of the handmaidens lends dignity to the decoy Queen as she holds court.

Feather headdress

Gemstone and filigree ear covering

Hood to hide face

Amidala disguised as a handmaiden

Sabé

The most important handmaiden is Sabé. First in line to become the royal decoy in times of danger, she dresses as the Queen and hides her features with white makeup. Amidala has coached Sabé in regal bearing and speech. Even so, she plays the role with apprehension, concerned that a subtle slip will give her sovereign away.

Luggage container   *Wardrobe container*

TRAVELING IN STYLE
The Royal Starship is equipped with wardrobe containers. From these containers, the handmaidens choose an elaborate dress for the Queen's appearance before the Senate.

Micrograv activates when container is closed

Accessory holders   *Climate-controled interior*

Travel luggage

The special wardrobe containers holding the Queen's wardrobe and jewelry include micrograv devices in their bases. These mechanisms ensure that clothes hang properly even if the closed container is tipped on its side.

Battle Dress

In her guise as the Queen, Sabé wears a distinctive battle dress that allows her maximum freedom of movement. In the palace throne room, Sabe's disguise fools the Neimoidian viceroy and allows Amidala to reach a hidden pistol.

Broad waistband

Surcoat

Long skirt made of blast-damping fabric

Medium-range barrel

Snap-action trigger

Power cell in grip

ROYAL PISTOL
After being selected, the handmaidens were given bodyguard training. Each is capable of using a pistol to help defend the Queen in the unlikely event of a disturbance or emergency.

Shiraya fan headdress worn only by Queen Amidala

Wide cowl masks Eirtaé's face

Gown decorated with the royal insignia

Veda pearl beading

Glass filaments

Rabé's simple gown sets off the majesty of the Queen's appearance

Eirtaé

Handmaiden Eirtaé comes from a town in a remote river valley. Her family was wealthy and she was taught the demands of etiquette. She helps the other handmaidens—and sometimes the Queen—with royal protocol.

Sabé (disguised as Amidala)

Rabé

Eirtaé

Saché

Yané

IN ATTENDANCE
Just as Amidala wears a particular dress for each different official occasion, the handmaidens dress in matching complementary clothes.

DATA FILE

◆ Amidala has five handmaidens: Rabé, Eirtaé, Sabé, Saché, and Yané.

◆ Rabé, Eirtaé, and Sabé accompany the Queen when she escapes Theed on the Royal Starship, while Saché and Yané reluctantly stay behind.

Padmé Naberrie

WHENEVER THE QUEEN is exposed to danger, she disguises herself as one of her own handmaidens, taking the name Padmé Naberrie. The identical hooded dresses and similar appearance of Amidala's handmaidens make it easy for Padmé to appear and disappear quietly from the group. When Padmé is among the attendants, handmaiden Sabé impersonates the Queen, subtly taking signals from Padmé regarding royal decisions. Captain Panaka is behind the creation of Amidala's double identity, having explained the old Palace scheme to her upon her coronation. In her guise as Padmé, Amidala accompanies Qui-Gon Jinn to Mos Espa to see for herself what the Jedi is up to.

Simple braids

Rough-spun cloth

Glass jewel of little value

In Mos Espa, the disguised Queen finds Qui-Gon Jinn's risky plans not to her liking but she cannot use her regal authority to object. Nonetheless, she realizes that the Jedi Master has the benefit of long experience, and she goes along with his scheme while harboring her doubts.

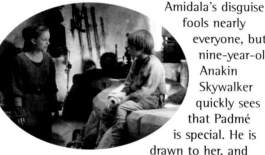

Amidala's disguise fools nearly everyone, but nine-year-old Anakin Skywalker quickly sees that Padmé is special. He is drawn to her, and she returns his affection, not quite knowing what to make of the gifted young boy.

Peasant Dress

When Qui-Gon Jinn determines to go into Mos Espa, Padmé decides to keep an eye on him. Captain Panaka, the Naboo Head of Security, promises to look after the ship. Rough peasant clothing helps Padmé blend in as an anonymous farm girl.

Removing her white facepaint is a key element in the success of Amidala's disguise as Padmé. People are so accustomed to the Queen's formal royal appearance that they do not give ordinary-looking Padmé a second glance.

Traditional Tatooine sand symbols

Japor ivory wood snippet obtained by Anakin through trading

Jerba leather cord

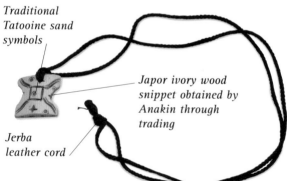

LUCKY CHARM
Knowing that the future is uncertain, especially his own, Anakin carves a good-luck charm for Padmé. He hopes that she will remember him by this token in spite of what may happen to each of them.

Wrist bindings keep out sand and dust

Plain walking boots

DATA FILE

◆ Padmé and Sabé practice indirect communication in private, making a game of speaking in cryptic ways. This practice makes it easier for Padmé to guide Sabé's actions as Queen.

◆ As humble Padmé, Amidala observes things that might not be revealed to the Queen.

Being disguised as Padmé robs Amidala of her regal power, but gives her the freedom to live as a normal person. In Mos Espa, she assists with Anakin's Podracer and helps out where needed.

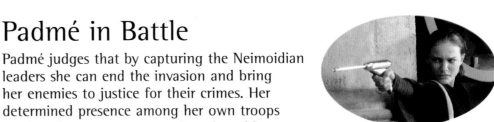

Padmé in Battle

Padmé judges that by capturing the Neimoidian leaders she can end the invasion and bring her enemies to justice for their crimes. Her determined presence among her own troops inspires them to success against the odds. Sabé remains disguised as the Queen to the end, providing Padmé with a critical advantage at the last minute.

MESSAGE FROM NABOO
While traveling to Coruscant, Padmé is tortured by the replay of Sio Bibble's hologram transmission, which tells of catastrophic death back on Naboo. Is it a trap? The truth? Or both? It takes great resolve for Padmé to stick to her plan of pleading Naboo's cause in the Galactic Senate when what she most wants is to be with her suffering people.

Hair pulled tightly back for action

High collar conceals blast-absorbing pad

Heavy cloth woven with energy-absorbing fibers to protect against blaster fire

Naboo royal emblem

Activator   _Encoder_   _Power cell_

Memory cell

Emitter/sensor tip

SIGNALLING UNIT

Minimal barrel makes blaster easy to hide

Smooth shell design allows blaster to be slipped out from concealment easily

Blaster gas cartridge cap

Snap trigger requires firm squeeze to prevent misfires

Energy cell in handgrip

Blaster

Padmé and the other handmaidens carry versions of the slim royal pistol. It is designed for practical use and easy concealment. The streamlined blasters pack a mild punch compared to true security guns, but they fire plasma bolts that can be deadly.

SECRET COMMUNICATION
Padmé uses a miniature device to transmit light and data signals silently to Captain Panaka during the battle in Theed.

Small, easily concealed blaster

Short-range barrel

Calf-length coatskirt protects legs and allows easy movement

RETURN TO THE PALACE
On her return to Naboo, Padmé dons battle dress. In the assault on her own palace, she fights alongside her troops and the Jedi allies in order to reach the throne room and confront the droid invaders. Braving onslaughts of laser bolts, Padmé is quick to return fire without qualms: she knows the battle droids are not living foes.

In Naboo's most desperate hour, Padmé reveals her secret identity to the Gungan ruler, Boss Nass. She knows that only a clear token of good faith such as this could win over the stubborn Gungan.

High-traction leather tactical boots

Sleeves cut for ease of movement

The Naboo

THE PEOPLE OF NABOO have prospered under the security of the Republic, advancing their society without concern for outside threats. Naboo is governed by an elected sovereign, a Governor, and an Advisory Council residing in the Royal Palace at the capital city of Theed. The Naboo live in cities and villages that are thinly scattered on the main landmass of their planet. A love of art is deeply seated in Naboo culture, taking such forms as grand architecture and elaborate clothing fashions. The Naboo regard their refined way of life as a birthright, but they will find that it is a luxury that they will have to defend.

NABOO
The planet Naboo is small, green, and honeycombed by a curious crustal substructure that is riddled with cave passages.

Formal collar

Fashionable Naboo sleeves and cuffs

THEED
The crown jewel of Naboo civilization is the city of Theed, built at the edge of a great plateau where the River Solleu winds its way toward a spectacular waterfall. Artisans, architects, and urban planners are all valued highly in Naboo culture, and their splendid city is a special testament to their efforts.

Sio Bibble

As governor of Naboo, the outspoken Sio Bibble oversees all matters brought to the Queen's attention. He also chairs the Advisory Council, and deals directly with regional representatives and town governing officials in day-to-day administration.

CULTURAL CAPITAL
In addition to the Royal Palace, the greatest Naboo libraries, museums, shrines, theaters, and conservatories are located in Theed. The city's buildings are designed in the classical Naboo style.

Domed roofs common on Naboo's buildings

Zoorif feather motif   NABOO JEWELRY   *Organic chif stone*

Sio Bibble is loath to concede to Captain Panaka's dire warnings of greater need for armament. A noble philosopher, he even refuses to change his mind during his planet's most desperate hour.

THE ADVISORY COUNCIL
The members of the Royal Advisory Council present matters to the Queen and offer her their expertise. The Council frequently changes the composition of its membership bringing a range of scholars, artists, and interested community members into the Queen's audience.

Formal hairstyle   *Robe of state*

HELA BRANDES
MUSIC ADVISOR

GRAF ZAPALO
MASTER OF SCIENCES

HUGO ECKENER
CHIEF ARCHITECT

LUFTA SHIF
EDUCATION REGENT

Philosopher's tunic

Governor's boots

Royal Starship

The gleaming Naboo Royal Starship conveys Queen Amidala to formal state appearances in matchless style. Built on Naboo using foreign-made engine and technology components, the ship blends the Naboo love of art with the industrial power available from other worlds.

ROYAL PERFECTION
The Royal Starship is quite unlike craft from other planets. Its distinctive interior is characterized by elegant curves and a clean, refined look. As with much Naboo design, utility is secondary to aesthetic concerns.

Hand-finished chromium finish is a royal prerogative

Starship carries no weapons

Throne room

Sublight engine

Heat sink finial makes fuel burn cleaner

High-resolution eyepiece

Talo-effect "lens" allows subatomic analysis

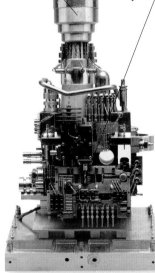

MESON TALOSCOPE

DAMAGE MONITOR
The Royal Starship has elaborate built-in systems to monitor equipment. When the ship suffers laser hits from the Trade Federation blockade, pilot Ric Olié can see at a glance exactly what has been damaged.

Enlarged section showing damage

Starship overview

View mode indicator allows different internal representations

HIGH-END INSTRUMENTS
High-precision diagnostic and analysis instruments onboard the Royal Starship allow the crew to conduct a variety of tests. The wide range of instruments is capable of anticipating problems before they occur.

Power cells pulse energy through equipment to be tested

Diagnostic block

Touch control

ENGINEERING ANALYSIS BOARD

DATA FILE

◆ Merchants on the fringes of Naboo's cities carry on a vital trade between their society and that of the Gungans.

◆ Onboard the Royal Starship, even simple components like this oscillation overthemister are handcrafted in the elegant Naboo style.

FORMAL FUTHARK
The Naboo alphabet has a traditional handwritten form, the futhork, and a formal form, called the futhark. The formal script, based on ovals, is used for purposes such as spacecraft identifications and control labels.

SOCIAL FABRIC
Clothing is often used as a form of social communication. During the Trade Federation blockade, citizens of Theed make subtle use of Naboo color and fashion symbolism to express their support or opposition to the Queen's policies.

Columns made of polished Naboo stone

Large windows lend serenity

Amidala seated before her Advisory Council

Theed Palace

Built centuries ago, the Royal Palace is the largest building in Theed. Its courts are used for meetings, dinners, parties, cultural events, and visiting dignitaries. The palace blends historic design facets with automatic doors, communications systems, and area-specific climate control.

Palace Guard

Composite holoprojector built into floor

Gestures of reassurance in the streets of Theed mask underlying tensions as people begin to grow hungry from the blockade. Some wonder whether their Queen will abandon them for her own safety.

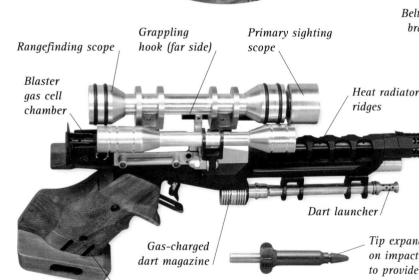

High officer headgear

Naboo Security crest

Captain Panaka

As Head of Security for Queen Amidala, Captain Panaka oversees every branch of the volunteer Royal Naboo Security Forces and is personally responsible for the Queen's safety. Panaka was appointed after his predecessor, Captain Magneta, failed to prevent the death of the former King Veruna, who had gone into hiding upon his abdication. Veruna's "accidental" death was covered up—even from the Queen—and Magneta quietly resigned. Panaka sees the increasingly dangerous state of affairs in the galaxy and argues for stronger security measures to protect the Queen and Naboo itself. Despite this, the Advisory Council convinces Amidala to act in accordance with Naboo's traditional pacifism. Panaka foresees the outcome of this noble policy, but it takes the terror of an invasion to bring his point home.

Panaka has the confidence of an experienced man and relies on his own judgment even when Jedi Knights step in. He believes that Qui-Gon Jinn's actions risk the Queen's safety and the fate of Naboo.

Leather jerkin covers thin anti-blast armor plates

Comlink in holster

Comlink attachment

Belt clip bracket

Sturdy casing

COMLINK HOLDER

Panaka's security forces use small ground craft like the Gian landspeeder for patrols and general operations. These light speeders are some of the few assets Panaka has in his effort to retake Theed Palace from the invading droids.

Rangefinding scope

Grappling hook (far side)

Primary sighting scope

Blaster gas cell chamber

Heat radiator ridges

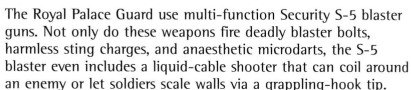

Voice pickup

Transmitter

Dart launcher

Gas-charged dart magazine

Tip expands on impact to provide firm anchorage

Handgrip

GRAPPLING HOOK

Heavy gripstock for firm control

Blaster

The Royal Palace Guard use multi-function Security S-5 blaster guns. Not only do these weapons fire deadly blaster bolts, harmless sting charges, and anaesthetic microdarts, the S-5 blaster even includes a liquid-cable shooter that can coil around an enemy or let soldiers scale walls via a grappling-hook tip.

COMLINK
Captain Panaka uses a master security comlink to keep in touch with his volunteer divisions, employing separate channels for command clarity.

Facing the Trade Federation forces, Panaka and his Palace Guard fight with determined efficiency to return the Queen to the throne.

Security Officer

Panaka's few top officers are loyal but mostly unfamiliar with real danger. During the Trade Federation invasion, they work hard to maintain order in Naboo.

Security Guard

Marshaled under the authority of Captain Panaka, the Security Guard is the closest thing to a regular infantry on Naboo. Individual Security Guards serve primarily as sentries and patrolmen in Theed, supplementing the Theed police force on behalf of the Royal Palace. Although well-drilled by Panaka, the Security Guard is no match for the mechanized army of the Trade Federation's invasion force.

Palace Guard

The Palace Guard is the highly-trained bodyguard of the Queen and court. While the Security Guard function as a militia, the Palace Guard is made up of dedicated soldiers who typically experience battle off-planet and return to protect the Queen out of loyalty. Although few in number, the Palace Guard is the backbone of Naboo security.

Officer's pistol

Officer's headgear

Wrist guard

Naboo Security crest

CR-2 basic blaster, built to last

Resilient armor plates

Combat helmet

Chin strap

Liquid cable shooter

Un-armored joints for agility

Utility belt

Leather jerkin

Utility belt

Blast-damping armor

No leg armor for mobility

Traditional full cut thigh

Studded forearm plate for hand-to-hand combat

Shin protectors buckle over short boots

Auxiliary gear straps

High-traction, quiet-soled security boots

Uniform color denotes Security Guard

Naboo Pilots

LIKE THEIR COMRADES the Security Guard and the Palace Guard, the Space Fighter Corps is a unit of the Royal Naboo Security Forces. Its pilots are a devil-may-care lot from diverse backgrounds who fly the custom-built Naboo N-1 Starfighters with pride. Their usual missions are routine patrols, escort duties, or parade flights. Lack of combat on peaceful Naboo forces the pilots to gain experience off-planet in Republic pirate fighter groups or on the rare patrol missions that encounter troublemakers. By no means the most dangerous bunch of space pilots in the galaxy, the Space Fighter Corps are nonetheless ready for action—even in the face of the Trade Federation's overwhelming challenge.

N-1 Starfighter

Partly finished in gleaming chromium to indicate royal status, N-1 starfighters sport radial engines of Nubian make in a J-configuration spaceframe. Assisted by an astromech droid, starfighters are fast and agile, but prone to uncontrollable spins when the engines suffer damage.

Flying goggles

Anti-glare brim

Built-in communicator system

Flying jacket

Space Fighter Corps overcoat

Pilot safety harness attaches to ship's seat

Bright colors typical of Naboo style

Flying gloves

Naboo pilot-issue boots

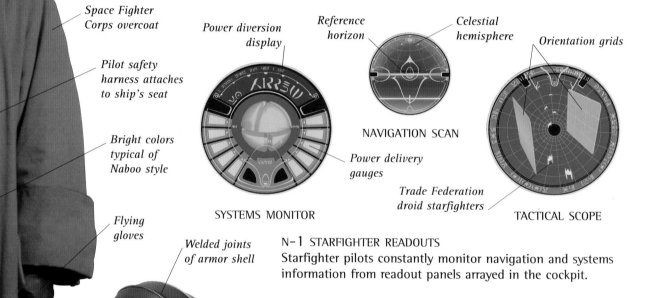

Power diversion display

Reference horizon

Celestial hemisphere

Orientation grids

Power delivery gauges

SYSTEMS MONITOR

NAVIGATION SCAN

Trade Federation droid starfighters

TACTICAL SCOPE

N-1 STARFIGHTER READOUTS
Starfighter pilots constantly monitor navigation and systems information from readout panels arrayed in the cockpit.

Welded joints of armor shell

Automatic distress beacon

FLYING HELMET

Ric Olié

The top pilot in the Space Fighter Corps is Ric Olié, a veteran flier who answers directly to Captain Panaka. Perfectly capable of flying any craft on Naboo, it is Ric Olié's honor to captain the Queen's Royal Starship. The run through the Trade Federation blockade taxes Olié's flying abilities to the limit, and even he doubts whether they can get through alive.

DATA FILE

◆ Naboo pilots must gain experience flying utility craft before they are permitted to take the controls of a coveted N-1 starfighter.

◆ Only a few lucky pilots have ever flown royal escort duty all the way to Coruscant, most never having left Naboo's sector.

R2-D2

DROID HOLD
In a small chamber on the lowest deck of the Naboo Royal Starship, R2-D2 recharges between work projects and waits with other astromech droids for assignments. A repulsorlift tube at one end of the hold conveys the droids to the outside of the ship for work on the hull during flight.

A UTILITY DROID with a mind of his own, there is more to R2-D2 than his ordinary appearance would suggest. Just one of several repair and maintenance droids assigned to the Naboo Royal Starship, R2-D2 replaces blown fuses, installs new wiring, polishes floors, and does whatever else is necessary to maintain the gleaming vessel in perfect working condition. For a utility droid, R2-D2 is equipped with remarkable tenacity and drive to accomplish his missions. Such dedication would ordinarily go unnoticed, but when crisis envelops the Royal Starship, R2-D2 becomes a hero.

Astromech droid repair-monitor image

R2-D2 at work on the hull

Damaged deflector shield generator

IN-FLIGHT REPAIRS
Astromech droids commonly carry out a wide variety of mechanical repair and information retrieval tasks. R2-D2 does not stand out from the crowd until he singlehandedly completes repairs to the Naboo Royal Starship's shield generator.

Secondary holographic projector

Primary photoreceptor and radar eye

CO-PILOT
Standard astromech droids are used in many space fighters as onboard flight support. R2-D2 accompanies Anakin Skywalker into battle in the droid socket of a Naboo N-1 Starfighter.

REPAIR ARM
This extendible arm can clean, cut, or seal electronic components.

Luminescent diagnostic display

Hydraulic extension arm

Optional oxidizer intake

Pneumatic cleaner

Sonic welder

ROCKET THRUSTER
Accessory rocket thrusters give R2 units the ability to propel themselves through air or space.

Hydraulic arm shaft

Heat exhaust

Thrust nozzle

Deployment brace

Control impulse and power net linkage

Inference pulse stabilizers

Sand-proof joints

DATA FILE

◆ R2-D2 is owned by the Royal House of Naboo. He was assigned to the Queen's ship because of his outstanding performance record.

◆ Artoo's head can telescope up so that he can see out of the tight neck of a Naboo Starfighter droid socket.

Extendible third leg

Swivel-mounted tread

All-terrain main drive tread

Powerbus cables

Jar Jar Binks

AN AMPHIBIOUS GUNGAN native to Naboo, Jar Jar is a luckless exile from his home city, Otoh Gunga. He now lives in the swamps, where he survives on his own, eating raw shellfish and other such swamp fare. His long muscular tongue helps him to scoop mollusks out of their shells and tasty gumbols out of their tree burrows. During the invasion of Naboo, Qui-Gon Jinn runs into and rescues Jar Jar. The simple Gungan's sense of honor binds him to Qui-Gon for life, even though the Jedi would much rather do without him at first.

At first, Obi-Wan Kenobi dismisses Jar Jar as an inconvenient life form to have around. However, the Gungan quickly proves useful by telling the Jedi of an underwater city where they can escape from the ground forces of the Trade Federation.

Gungan Survivor

Like all Gungans, Jar Jar's skeleton is made of cartilage, making him flexible and rubbery. Even his skull and jaws are elastic, giving the simple Gungan a wide range of facial expressions. Jar Jar's character, like his body, is resilient and able to bend to changes of fortune without letting his spirit break. Whether alone, in the company of Jedi, or even among royalty, Jar Jar blunders through life with light-hearted good humor in spite of his occasional panic attacks.

Jar Jar is reticent about the reason for his exile from Otoh Gunga, glossing over the fact that he accidentally flooded most of Boss Nass's mansion and several adjoining bubbles while working as a waiter at a high-class party. As this was not Jar Jar's first serious accident, or even his first serious flooding accident, Boss Nass was furious, and Jar Jar was exiled from his own city under pain of death.

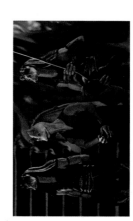

Jar Jar is well known to the city patrol of Otoh Gunga, which has extricated him from all kinds of trouble in the past—from petty squabbles over food theft to the commotion Jar Jar caused when he inadvertently opened half of the Otoh Gunga Zoo bubbles. They know Boss Nass will not be pleased to see the infamous Gungan in his chambers again.

Partially retractable eyestalk

Nictitating membrane

Nostrils seal underwater

Large teeth for cracking shellfish

Tough skin near head for burrowing

Haillu (earlobes) for display

Tight vocal cords produce high-pitched voice

Lanky build from life in exile

Mottled skin for camouflage

Fashion statement

Mollusk and gumbol breakfast

GUNGAN HANDCUFFS

Four-fingered hand

Cartilaginous skeleton is stiff but not brittle

When Qui-Gon Jinn goes to Mos Espa in search of hyperdrive parts, Jar Jar accompanies him. Qui-Gon knows that this odd Gungan will help him blend into the diverse population of strange life forms inhabiting the city. Meanwhile, Jar Jar worries about exposing his amphibian skin to the heat and suns.

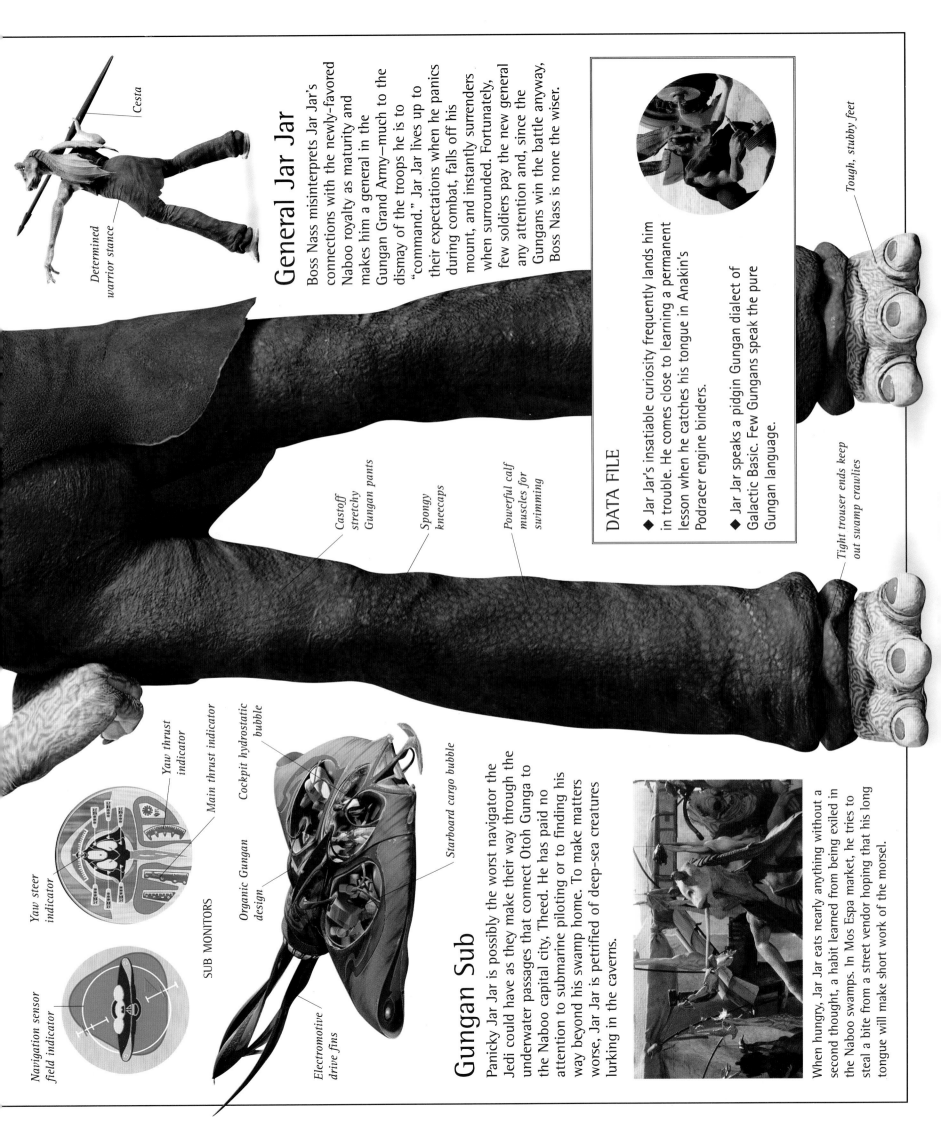

Cesta

Determined warrior stance

General Jar Jar

Boss Nass misinterprets Jar Jar's connections with the newly-favored Naboo royalty as maturity and makes him a general in the Gungan Grand Army—much to the dismay of the troops he is to "command." Jar Jar lives up to their expectations when he panics during combat, falls off his mount, and instantly surrenders when surrounded. Fortunately, few soldiers pay the new general any attention and, since the Gungans win the battle anyway, Boss Nass is none the wiser.

DATA FILE

◆ Jar Jar's insatiable curiosity frequently lands him in trouble. He comes close to learning a permanent lesson when he catches his tongue in Anakin's Podracer engine binders.

◆ Jar Jar speaks a pidgin Gungan dialect of Galactic Basic. Few Gungans speak the pure Gungan language.

Tough, stubby feet

Tight trouser ends keep out swamp crawlies

Castoff stretchy Gungan pants

Spongy kneecaps

Powerful calf muscles for swimming

Yaw thrust indicator

Main thrust indicator

Cockpit hydrostatic bubble

Yaw steer indicator

Starboard cargo bubble

SUB MONITORS

Navigation sensor field indicator

Organic Gungan design

Electromotive drive fins

Gungan Sub

Panicky Jar Jar is possibly the worst navigator the Jedi could have as they make their way through the underwater passages that connect Otoh Gunga to the Naboo capital city, Theed. He has paid no attention to submarine piloting or to finding his way beyond his swamp home. To make matters worse, Jar Jar is petrified of deep-sea creatures lurking in the caverns.

When hungry, Jar Jar eats nearly anything without a second thought, a habit learned from being exiled in the Naboo swamps. In Mos Espa market, he tries to steal a bite from a street vendor hoping that his long tongue will make short work of the morsel.

The Gungans

GUNGANS EVOLVED in the swamps of Naboo, becoming almost equally well adapted to life on land and in water. The amphibious beings live in underwater cities hidden in deep lakes, breathing air or water with their compound lungs. Secret techniques allow Gungans to "grow" the basic structures of buildings and vehicles, which are complemented and finished by Gungan artisans in organic styles. Gungans trade with the Naboo for certain items of technology, but manufacture everything else they need from the resources of their underwater habitat. Although Gungans use mechanized vehicles, they have a close affinity with the natural world and still prefer to utilize living mounts and beasts of burden.

Older Gungans have hairlike finlets

Whiskers indicate maturity

Hydrostatic bubbles of Otoh Gunga

Kernode assembly for larger bubbles

Hydrostatic field

Atmospheric purifiers

Field utanode assembly

Utanode

Captain Tarpals

Kaadu patrol chief in Otoh Gunga, Captain Tarpals is usually on the lookout for thieves or dangerous water creatures that might threaten the Gungan populace. To the weary Tarpals, accident-prone Jar Jar Binks is a familiar menace who occupies his own special category.

Minimal utanode construction requires high power draw

Root counterphase array

Backup generator

Stabilizer

Portal zone

Generators

Field wave stabilizer

Utanode assembly brace

Habitation floor

Counterphase harmonizing struts

Otoh Gunga

The magical gleam of Otoh Gunga is hidden in the deep waters of Lake Paonga. Powerful hydrostatic membrane fields keep water out of the dwelling bubbles and give the city its characteristic jewel-like look. Special portal zones hold air in and allow Gungans to pass through without needing to use an airlock.

Field focusing element

Hydrostatic field generators

Scalefish

A variety of small fish coexist in the waters around Otoh Gunga. They are drawn to the city by its lights, but have learned by experience not to pass through to the air-filled interior.

Poison spine

RAY

TEE

LAA

FAA

MEE

SEE

Boss Nass

Mangana aqua jewel

Crown of rulership

Prosperous face

Epaulets of military authority

Ruler of Otoh Gunga, the largest lake city, Boss Nass is a stern, old-fashioned Gungan who speaks Galactic Basic with a strong accent. He commands great authority even in communities beyond Otoh Gunga and has grown large and prosperous in his advancing years. It is in Boss Nass's power alone to summon the Gungan Grand Army, which is made up of Gungans from all settlements.

Swirl designs typical of Otoh Gungan clothing

Four-fingered hand

Rep hood

Rep robe

A fair but stubborn ruler, Boss Nass resents the arrogance of the Naboo, who regard Gungans as primitive simply because they do not embrace a technological lifestyle. He finds it best all around to minimize contact with humans.

Otoh swirls

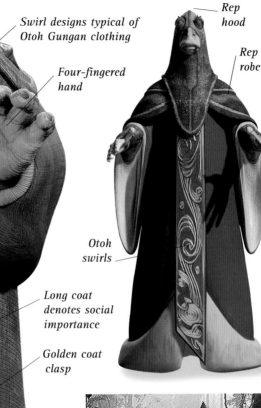

Long coat denotes social importance

Golden coat clasp

Rep Teers

Boss Nass makes decisions with the assistance of his Rep Council. This group of appointed officers is responsible for various areas of government. Their special clothing indicates the dignity of their office. Rep Teers is responsible for the power supply that sustains the hydrostatic bubbles of Otoh Gunga.

Like all the Naboo, Queen Amidala was taught to think of Gungans as barbarians. But when the planet is faced with invasion, she realizes that her people and the Gungans must work together or die. Humbly finding the courage to ask Boss Nass for help, Amidala forges a new friendship between the two cultures. Deeply impressed with her gesture, Boss Nass changes his views as well.

Gungan sandals

DATA FILE

◆ Boss Nass has the distinctive green skin and hooded eyes of the old Ankura lineage that hails from an isolated swamp village. His distant ancestors united with the Otolla Gungans who founded Otoh Gunga.

◆ Keeper of ancient records, Rep Been knows the secrets of old Gungan hiding places.

Gungan Warfare

LONG UNITED by treaties, the Gungans do not fight the Naboo or each other. Many years ago they drove off the last invaders to threaten them. Nonetheless they maintain an armed force for tradition and defense against attack by sea monsters. The Grand Army employs both technological wizardry and traditional weaponry. Its primary focus is on defense, for which animal-mounted shield generators are used. For attack, the Gungans hurl plasmic energy balls. Soldiers of the Grand Army are inexperienced, but their resolve comes from a firm sense of duty and justice.

Emerging from the swamps, Gungan troops from all the underwater communities unite by stages into the single body of the Grand Army. Gungan soldiers know that they must face the Trade Federation army to ensure their people's survival and freedom.

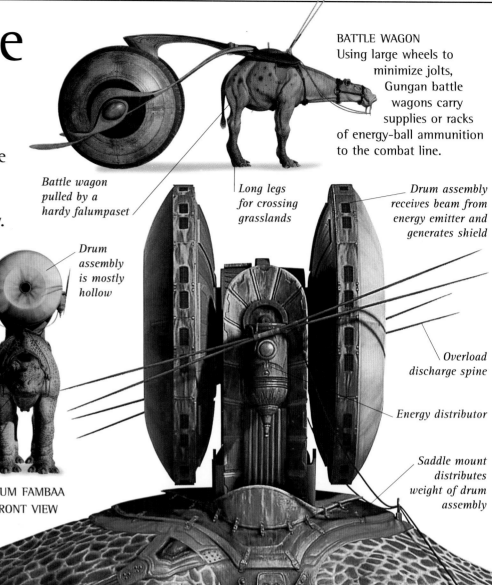

BATTLE WAGON
Using large wheels to minimize jolts, Gungan battle wagons carry supplies or racks of energy-ball ammunition to the combat line.

Battle wagon pulled by a hardy falumpaset

Long legs for crossing grasslands

Drum assembly receives beam from energy emitter and generates shield

Drum assembly is mostly hollow

Drum fambaa aligns with beam fambaa in front

DRUM FAMBAA
FRONT VIEW

Overload discharge spine

Energy distributor

Saddle mount distributes weight of drum assembly

Giant goff bird feathers

CAVALRY
The Grand Army consists mostly of militiagungs, or part-time soldiers. Individuals provide their own uniforms, resulting in some variation in gear and clothing.

Saddlehorn

Kaadu

Kaadu were domesticated long ago by Gungans who then lived on the surface of Naboo. They are primarily adapted for land-dwelling but can also breathe underwater for long periods. Kaadu decorated with giant feathers serve as agile mounts for Gungan soldiers and scouts.

DATA FILE

◆ Fambaa shield generators heat up when under fire and can be used only for a limited time under heavy attack.

◆ Signals and orders are transmitted by horns, as well as by gestures and whistles.

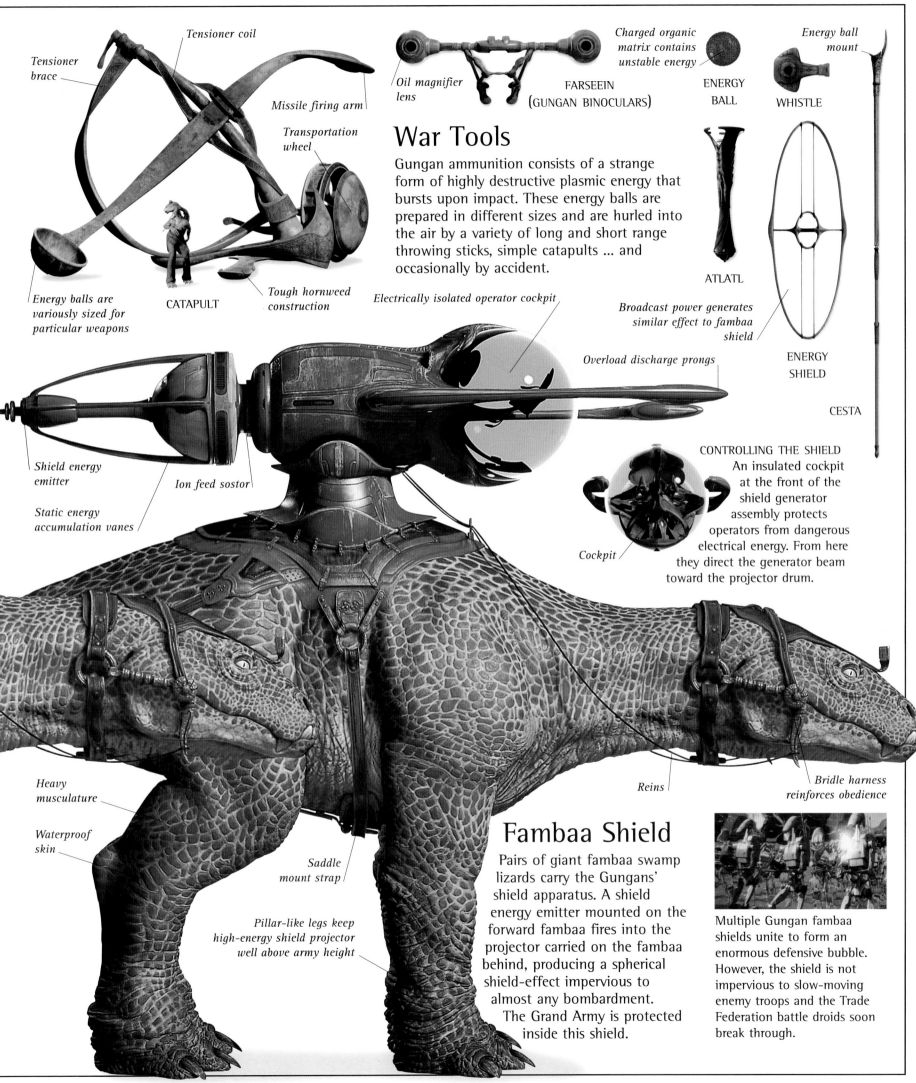

Tensioner brace

Tensioner coil

Missile firing arm

Transportation wheel

Oil magnifier lens

FARSEEIN (GUNGAN BINOCULARS)

Charged organic matrix contains unstable energy

ENERGY BALL

Energy ball mount

WHISTLE

Energy balls are variously sized for particular weapons

CATAPULT

Tough hornweed construction

ATLATL

War Tools

Gungan ammunition consists of a strange form of highly destructive plasmic energy that bursts upon impact. These energy balls are prepared in different sizes and are hurled into the air by a variety of long and short range throwing sticks, simple catapults ... and occasionally by accident.

Broadcast power generates similar effect to fambaa shield

ENERGY SHIELD

CESTA

Electrically isolated operator cockpit

Overload discharge prongs

Shield energy emitter

Ion feed sostor

Static energy accumulation vanes

CONTROLLING THE SHIELD
An insulated cockpit at the front of the shield generator assembly protects operators from dangerous electrical energy. From here they direct the generator beam toward the projector drum.

Cockpit

Heavy musculature

Waterproof skin

Saddle mount strap

Reins

Bridle harness reinforces obedience

Pillar-like legs keep high-energy shield projector well above army height

Fambaa Shield

Pairs of giant fambaa swamp lizards carry the Gungans' shield apparatus. A shield energy emitter mounted on the forward fambaa fires into the projector carried on the fambaa behind, producing a spherical shield-effect impervious to almost any bombardment.
The Grand Army is protected inside this shield.

Multiple Gungan fambaa shields unite to form an enormous defensive bubble. However, the shield is not impervious to slow-moving enemy troops and the Trade Federation battle droids soon break through.

Sea Monsters of Naboo

THE WATERS OF NABOO are rich with life, the balance of sunlight and nutrients being ideal for many life forms. Microscopic plankton flourish in prodigious numbers, supporting a food chain that reaches its peak in giant predators. The sea monsters of Naboo are primarily lurkers of the deep, but some are known to drift to the surface at night or during storms—making ship travel a proverbially bad idea on the planet. Some of these monstrous creatures have been known to prey upon Gungan cities in oddly coordinated attacks, which is partly why the Gungan army stands in continued readiness. Repellent fields keep the leviathans away from the cities most of the time, but for still unexplained reasons one occasionally swims through.

Tail highly sensitive to movement

Luminescent skin patterns help lure prey

Newborn colo claw fish are fully-equipped instinctive hunters

BABY COLO CLAW FISH

GUNGAN SUB TRAVELING THROUGH THE CORE

Organs of unknown purpose at end of tail

Long tail provides propulsion

Rayed tail flukes

Opee Sea Killer

A bizarre amalgam of traits ordinarily found only in a range of disparate creatures, the opee sea killer clings within dark crags, using a lure on its head to draw the attention of potential prey. It then pursues the prey using a combination of swimming legs and jet propulsion. The opee sucks in water through its mouth and emits it through openings under the plates in its skin, allowing strikingly fast swimming speeds. When the prey is near enough, the opee shoots out its long, sticky tongue.

Lure

Jet propulsion vents

Pectoral fins for guidance

Multidirectional eyestalks

Tough body plates

Gungan Sub

Tail legs drive water and help the opee cling motionless in rocky crags, waiting for prey

Opee sea killers are both aggressive and persistent. Even when attacked by large predators, these ferocious killers refuse to give up, and young opees have been known to chew their way out of a colo claw fish's belly.

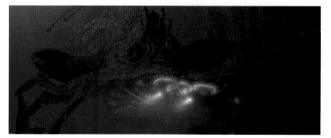

Shriek chords · Angling lures · Poisonous fangs

Stomach stretches to accommodate prey

Distensible jaw

Grasping claw

Colo Claw Fish

This serpentine predator is adapted to swallow prey larger than its own head. Its jaws can distend and its skin can stretch to engulf astonishingly large creatures. The colo seizes a prey with the huge pectoral claws for which it is named, having initially disoriented it by uttering a weird hydrosonic shriek using special structures in its throat and head. The colo digests its food slowly using weak stomach acids and must be certain to stun its prey with its venomous fangs before swallowing to avoid the creature eating its way out of the colo to safety.

Muscular body not smoothed by fat or blubber, and not fully adapted to swimming

Non-streamlined head evidence of land-based ancestor

Strong jaws for powerful bite

Eye

Gills   Mouth

Webbed hands allow the monster to grasp its prey

Investigating the habits of the sando aqua monster would be a highly dangerous undertaking, even using the most advanced defensive equipment. The sando appears without warning and can swallow most other sea dwellers in a single gulp.

Sando Aqua Monster

The most fabled of Naboo's sea nightmares, the sando aqua monster is rarely seen. In spite of its awesome size, it is somehow capable of hiding in deep environments. The sando aqua monster's arms and legs are only partly adapted into flippers, which suggests that its recent ancestors must have been land creatures. How this gargantuan beast eats enough to support its body functions remains to be explained—as does much of Naboo's ecology.

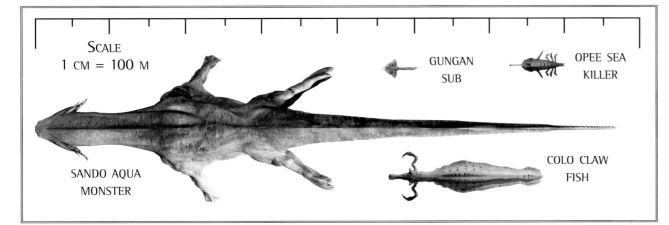

SCALE
1 CM = 100 M

GUNGAN SUB

OPEE SEA KILLER

SANDO AQUA MONSTER

COLO CLAW FISH

The opee sea killer's armored body protects it against most underwater predators, but it is defenseless against the powerful jaws of giant leviathans such as the sando aqua monster.

Darth Maul

Transmission antenna

Scan-absorbing stealth shell

Magnetic imaging device

FUELED BY THE AGGRESSIVE energies of the dark side, the Sith order began almost two millennia ago with a renegade Jedi who sought to use the Force to gain control. Both strengthened and twisted by the dark side, the Sith fought against each other to gain power and domination until only one remained: Darth Bane. To prevent internecine strife, Bane remade the Sith as an order that would endure in only two individuals at a time. Biding their time, the Sith lay in wait for the right moment to overturn the Jedi and seize control of the galaxy. The present Sith Master, Darth Sidious is the diabolically brilliant mind behind the training of one of the most dangerous Sith apprentices in history: the deadly Darth Maul.

Darth Sidious uses a clear and powerful hologram transmission to communicate with his Neimoidian minions and his apprentice field agent, Darth Maul. Fiercely demanding of high standards, Sidious has been known to dismiss individuals simply for communicating with too weak a signal.

Thermal imager

External weapons mount

Primary photoreceptor

Levitator

Light-gathering lens

Multi-scan controls

Power cells

Electrobinoculars

On Tatooine, Maul uses electrobinoculars to search for the Jedi. These electrobinoculars are equipped with radiation sensors for night vision and powerful light-gathering components for long distance scanning.

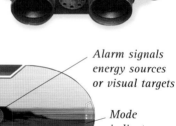

Probe Droid

Darth Maul uses elaborate technology in his work as the Sith apprentice of Darth Sidious. One of his most useful tools is the "dark eye" probe droid, a hovering reconnaissance device that can be programmed to seek out individuals or information.

"DARK EYE" DEVICES
Probe droids locate their quarry using multispectral imaging and many kinds of scanning. The probes silently monitor conversations and eavesdrop on electronic transmissions, and can be fitted with a number of small, deadly weapons.

Memory stores 360° horizon view

Filters screen out atmospheric interference

Nav-grid can be projected onto landscape

Range to target

Alarm signals energy sources or visual targets

Mode indicator

Magnification

ELECTROBINOCULAR VIEWSCREEN
Tied to global mapping scanners in his starship, Maul's electrobinocular viewscreen displays the precise location of targets and indicates life signals or power frequencies. Specific shapes, colors, or energy types can be set as targets, and even invisible defensive fields can be detected.

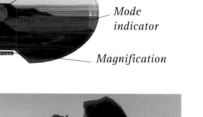

Maul prides himself on his abilities as a tracker, and relishes the challenge of difficult assignments given to him by his Sith master.

Scanning lens attachment

Ball detonator

Braking pedals

Acceleration handgrips

Steering bar

Open cockpit design offers optimum visibility

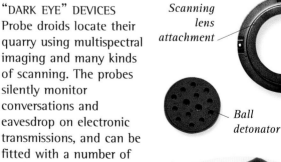

Darth Maul's speeder is powered by a strong repulsorlift engine for rapid acceleration and sharp cornering. The open-cockpit design allows Maul to leap directly from the speeder into battle.

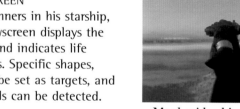

Repulsorlift

SITH SPEEDER
The speeder carries no weapons, since Maul prefers the direct assault of blade weapons or the treachery of bombs to the use of blasters.

Sith Apprentice

Vestigial horns

Hairless skull

Face tattoos

Gleaming yellow eyes

Darth Maul is one of the most highly trained Sith in the history of the order. Focusing on physical and tactical abilities, Maul serves his master obediently, knowing that his own time for strategic wisdom and eventual domination will come. His face is tattooed with symbols giving evidence of his complete dedication to discipline in the dark side.

With his double-bladed lightsaber, Maul is equal to two Jedi who are unprepared for his powers. Since the Sith disappeared almost 2,000 years ago, Jedi are not used to facing opponents with lightsabers.

Dark robe

Blade projection plate

Activator

Control lock

Blade modulation control

Control lock

Gauntlets

Maul's weapon is two joined lightsabers

Ribbed handgrip

Blade modulation circuitry

Double-bladed lightsaber

Beam emitter

Field cloak cut to allow fighting movement

Lightsaber blade is red due to nature of internal crystals

Heavy-action boots

Transmission and reception antenna

Function controls

WRIST LINK

Darth Maul's programmable wrist link allows him to remotely direct "dark eye" probe droids, arm traps, detonate bombs, and conduct other treacherous activities. It also receives signals from surveillance devices.

Maul's Lightsaber

Pushing his physical and Force-assisted abilities to the utmost, Darth Maul built and uses a double-bladed lightsaber as his primary weapon. Traditionally used only as a training device, the double-ended saber can be much more dangerous to its wielder than an enemy. In the hands of Darth Maul, however, it becomes a whirling vortex of lethal energy.

DATA FILE

◆ Maul's lightsaber contains two sets of internal components; one can act as backup to the other.

◆ Darth Maul's Sith Infiltrator spaceship is equipped with a rare cloaking device, allowing him to travel invisibly.

Anakin Skywalker

ALTHOUGH HE MAY LOOK like any other nine-year-old boy living on the Outer Rim desert planet of Tatooine, Anakin Skywalker is far from ordinary. A slave to the junk dealer Watto, Anakin lives with his mother in the spaceport city of Mos Espa. He has a natural ability with mechanical devices, quickly understanding how they work. In his spare time, Anakin repairs and builds machines, including Podracer engines and a working droid. Qui-Gon Jinn notices his keen perception and unnaturally fast reflexes, and recognizes that the Force is extraordinarily strong in Anakin.

Adjustable goggles

Connection plate

Headphones

Leather neck wrap

PODRACER POWER CELL

No human has ever needed a Podracing helmet in Mos Espa, since humans ordinarily cannot ride Podracers. Anakin's extra-small helmet was made for him as a gift by Taieb, a local craftsman.

Protective magnifier eyeplate

WELDING GOGGLES

Family and Friends

Anakin's mother, Shmi, believes in Anakin and encourages him in his dreams to escape slavery on Tatooine. His best friend, Kitster, is a fellow slave who hopes someday to become a majordomo for a wealthy Mos Espa estate. Anakin's unusual talents sometimes distance him from his friends, but Kitster has always been loyal.

Necklace given to Anakin by his mother

Slave's simple haircut

KITSTER

Among Anakin's friends is Wald, a young Rodian who speaks Huttese. Wald doubts Anakin's extraordinary abilities.

Tool pouch

Survival flares for use in sandstorms

Leg wraps keep out sand

Cheap, durable jumba leather

TRAVEL LUGGAGE

WUPIUPI (TATOOINE COINS)

Anakin has his own room in the Skywalker home. Electronic and mechanical components are piled around his bed since Anakin is constantly tinkering and trying to figure things out. Working for Watto gives Anakin opportunities for picking up scrap equipment here and there.

Arm wraps

Slave and Dreamer

Anakin has been raised by his mother to believe in himself. She has given him faith in his dreams in spite of their humble situation as slaves. Anakin looks forward to the day when he will be free to pilot starships of the mainline through the spacelanes of the galaxy. He soon finds that belief in one's dreams can have powerful results.

Rough work clothing

DATA FILE

◆ Anakin once belonged to Gardulla the Hutt, but she lost him in a bet to Watto when Anakin was about three years old.

◆ As a nine-year-old boy, Anakin would never be allowed to compete in civilized Podraces, but the Outer Rim is known for its exciting free-for-all race policies.

Air scoops act as
steering brakes

Radon-Ulzer
engines

Thrust
stabilizer cone

Control cable

Control Pod

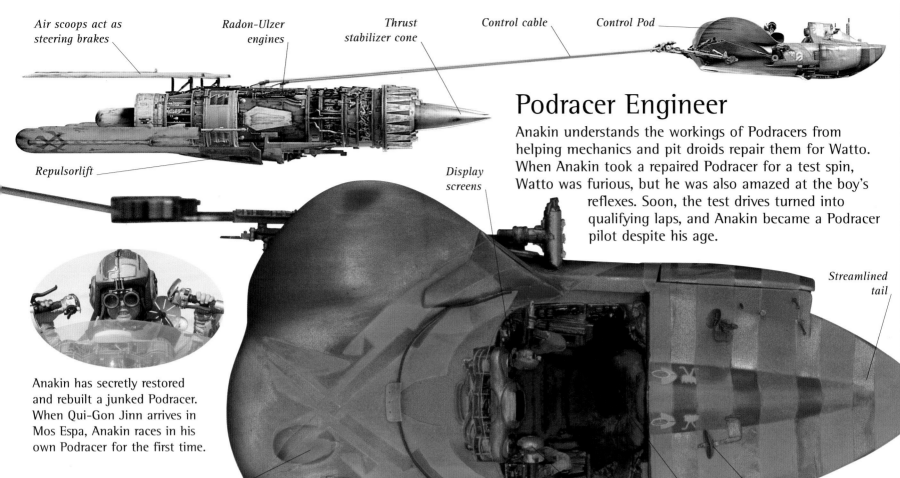

Repulsorlift

Display
screens

Podracer Engineer

Anakin understands the workings of Podracers from
helping mechanics and pit droids repair them for Watto.
When Anakin took a repaired Podracer for a test spin,
Watto was furious, but he was also amazed at the boy's
reflexes. Soon, the test drives turned into
qualifying laps, and Anakin became a Podracer
pilot despite his age.

Streamlined
tail

Anakin has secretly restored
and rebuilt a junked Podracer.
When Qui-Gon Jinn arrives in
Mos Espa, Anakin races in his
own Podracer for the first time.

Racing graphics painted by
R2-D2 under C-3PO's direction

Streamlined air scoop fender

Power-cell
access
hatch

Control
linkage brace

Throttle
levers

Pilot's
seat

Telemetry
transmitter

Hydraulic pressure charging system

Schematic view of
engine mid-systems

Pressure
management
mode indicator

Acceleration rate
indicator

Interval
velocity scale

Highlighted
system near
critical level

Overpressure
alarm

ANAKIN'S PODRACER DISPLAYS

Starfighter Pilot

One of Anakin's dreams is to become
a starfighter pilot, and he practises in
simulator games whenever possible. Most of
Anakin's friends think his dreams are unrealistic, but
a few people realize that there is something special
about him. During the invasion of Naboo, Anakin
hides in a starfighter cockpit half-knowing that he
might try it out ... just a little.

When the starfighter autopilot
engages, the ship flies Anakin
into the heart of the battle
raging above. He must think
furiously fast to figure out the
controls before he is killed.

When his dreams start coming
true faster than he can keep up,
Anakin finds himself standing in
the center of the Jedi Council
Chamber on Coruscant. Yoda
believes that the boy is too old,
angry, and fearful to begin Jedi
training. But Anakin is determined
not to be underestimated.

Crash-landing deep within the
Trade Federation Droid Control
Ship, Anakin accidentally fires
his torpedoes into the pilot
reactors, setting off a
cataclysmic chain reaction.

Shmi Skywalker

WHEN PIRATES CAPTURED her parents during a space voyage in the Outer Rim, young Shmi Skywalker was sold into slavery and separated from her family. During a difficult childhood, Shmi was taken from one system to another by several masters of various species while serving as a house servant. When no longer a girl, Shmi was dropped from house servant status and was forced into cleaning work. Although slavery is illegal in the Republic, laws do not reach all parts of the galaxy—and while inexpensive droids can perform menial tasks as well as humans, living slaves give great status and prestige to their owners.

Simple hairstyle typical of servants

Rough-spun tunic withstands harsh Tatooine weather

Decorative belt

WORKSTATION
When Shmi is not working at Watto's home, she is permitted to clean computer memory devices to bring in a modest income. A small area in their home where Shmi keeps her tools and equipment is devoted to this activity.

Aeromagnifier

Some of the tools at Shmi's workstation were given to Shmi in recognition of her service as a dependable servant. When Watto obtained an aeromagnifier in a large lot of used goods, he gave it to Shmi even though he could have sold it. The magnifier hovers in the right position to help her see what she is working on.

Repulsor hood

Mladong bracelet

Illuminator rings

Magnifier

SHMI'S KITCHEN
In spite of their poverty, Shmi works hard to make a good home for herself and her son, Anakin. Her kitchen includes some labor-saving devices, but lacks the more costly moisture-conserving domes and fields, which help save precious—and expensive—water.

Spicy ahrisa *Lamta* *Haroun bread* *Sidi gourd*

MOS ESPA PRODUCE *Tezirett seed* *Driss pod*

Slave and Mother

Tantalized several times by the false possibility of freedom, Shmi now accepts her life and finds joy in her son Anakin, whom she loves dearly. Shmi and Anakin live together in the Slave Quarter of Mos Espa, a collection of adobe hovels piled together at the edge of town.

When the Jedi Master Qui-Gon Jinn recognizes Anakin's special qualities and offers to take him away to a greater destiny, only Shmi's selfless care for her son gives her the strength to let him go.

DATA FILE

◆ Shmi learned her technical skills under a former master, Pi-Lippa, who planned to grant Shmi her freedom. However, when Pi-Lippa died Shmi was sold to a relative.

◆ Shmi can always sense when Anakin is nearby, even when she cannot see or hear him.

C-3PO

STANDARD CYBOT GALACTICA protocol droids have been in use for generations. When Anakin Skywalker found the structural elements of a droid that had been scavenged for parts, he restored it as a helper for his mother. Over time, Anakin scrounged the parts to complete his droid, fabricating many components and wiring sets himself. Anakin's droid lacks a "skin" since usable droid plating is valuable and the boy cannot afford it. The hapless droid, which Anakin calls C-3PO, has yet to realize that all his parts are showing.

Balance gyro

Borrowed photoreceptors

Vocoder plate

Movement sensor wiring

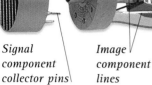

Photoreceptor mount frame

Composite image integrator

Image signal transmitter

Signal component collector pins

Image component lines

Photoreceptor modulation impulse carrier

Active sensing elements

Photoreceptor elements

PHOTORECEPTOR FRONT VIEW

Photoreceptor

The old droid frame Anakin started with had burned-out photoreceptors. Anakin switched these for the eyes of a used droid bought by Watto—which can now barely see. Watto still hasn't figured out how the half-blind droid managed to walk into his shop in the first place.

Rack for micro-tools

TOOL DEMAGNETIZER

Component schematic plans

ANAKIN'S TOOLS
On Tatooine, many devices are ruined by sand and dust and then thrown away. Anakin and Shmi look out for such castoffs, which they use in their work at home.

DIAGNOSTIC SCREEN

Main power recharge socket

Pelvic joint

Flexible mid-body section

While Anakin has tinkered with small devices for years, C-3PO is his first fully functional droid. Building a droid, even from standardized components, can be a challenge.

Magnetic rotation assembly links to actuating coupler

Lubricant circulation conduit

Auxiliary lubrication system pressurizer

High-torque knee joint

Intermotor actuating coupler

Structural limb strut

Foot angle sensor

HIGH-TORQUE MOTOR

Rotating pin anchors into limb

Sturdy mount pole

MICRO-CIRCUIT WELDER

Cleaner/ energizer

Welding stylus

DATA FILE

◆ Most of C-3PO's structural framework is more than 80 years old.

◆ C-3PO's programming includes memory banks that he draws upon to design the racing graphics for the cockpit of Anakin's Podracer. When he works on Anakin's machine, Threepio teams up with his future counterpart, R2-D2, for the first time.

Watto

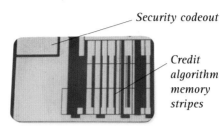

In the rugged frontier society of the Outer Rim, only hard currency counts. When Qui-Gon shows up hoping to pay with Republic credits, Watto only laughs.

SHREWD AND POSSESSIVE, Watto is the owner of a parts shop in the Tatooine frontier town of Mos Espa. A flying Toydarian with rapidly-beating wings, Watto's pudgy body is not as heavy as it looks due to his spongy, gas-filled tissues. The junk dealer has a sharp eye for a bargain, and knows equipment merchandise inside and out. Success has allowed Watto to indulge his passion for gambling. He regularly places large bets on Mos Espa's famous Podrace competitions, matching his wits and money against the Hutts, who control the gambling world. In the past, such bets have won Watto many slaves—prized possessions and trophies of his acumen.

Fast-beating wings allow Watto to hover

SERVING COUNTER
TEST PANELS

Security codeout

Credit algorithm memory stripes

REPUBLIC CREDIT CHIP

Watto's Junkshop

Although Watto insists that his establishment is a parts dealership, everyone else calls it a junk shop. It cannot be denied that the range of merchandise runs from desirable rare parts and working droids to unusable scrap that he would have a hard time unloading even on desperate Jawas. Watto's droids, slaves, and staff perform repairs, obtain parts needed by clients, and do custom work with a wide range of mechanical devices.

Old-style sales register device

Protocol droid (missing some parts)

Miscellaneous scrap stuck to short-range re-grav plate in ceiling

Pit droid

Power droids handy for powering up depleted cells in merchandise

Rough adobe walls hide coolant circulating layers

Hard memory cycler (cleaned by Shmi Skywalker)

Illuminated counter surface

Electrostatic damping floor mats keep sand and dust down

Monocular photoreceptor

Equipment interface panel

Bizarre improvised equipment can be found in Watto's shop, such as the Jawa R1-type drone that assists with shopkeeping.

Serving arms

Diagnostic hookup for testing trade merchandise

Charger plug

Cipher converter module

Touch keys

Data readout screen

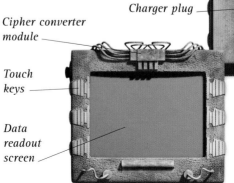

WATTO'S DATAPAD
Watto has an amazing memory for the inventory of his shop, but is careful to maintain accounting records in a special cipher using a sturdy datapad.

Power Droid

Power droids of the GNK series are mobile generators that supply power for machinery or other droids. They hover silently in the background, so commonplace that they are hardly noticed.

Monochromatic photoreceptor

Polyfeed power outlets

Ambulation gear housing

Vocoder

TALKING MAGNETITE CLEANER

Three-fingered hand

Dubious squint

Flexible trunklike nose

Three-day stubble

HIGH-OCTANE HOVERING
Watto's wings can beat as fast as ten times a second, burning up huge reserves of energy. To fuel his intense body functions, the Toydarian eats concentrated foods and imported egg-seeds.

DIRTY DEALING
Watto is not above using loaded chance cubes to give him an edge in his bargaining. He rolls his cubes to decide which slave to give Qui-Gon Jinn—Anakin or his mother, Shmi. However, the Jedi plays a loaded game, too, using mind powers to force the cube to favor Anakin.

Fashion statement

Belt straps

Keycodes for main safe and slave keepers

Pudgy belly mostly composed of gas

AT THE RACES
A favorite diversion of Watto's is watching Podraces from his fine seating box at Mos Espa Grand Arena. Nonhuman friends and acquaintances fill the box with passionate race-fan enthusiasm, as well as the vain prayers and curses of any gambling crowd.
It is the thrill of the races and the society of like-minded enthusiasts that keep Watto firmly at home on Tatooine.

Toydarian
The food-rich muck lakes of Watto's homeworld are filled with grabworms and other predators, making the ability to hover valuable for survival. When a safe landing is assured, Toydarian webbed feet spread out to make walking over slushy algae mats easier.

Datapad

Adjustable pocket welding torch

Welding tips and brazing bars

Welding torch power cord

Odor vaporizer

Refill cap

Solution reservoirs

THE GOOD LIFE
Watto enjoys smoking from a shisha oil-pipe, which mottles his skin and makes it even baggier. He uses scenters to recreate on Tatooine the algae-mat ambiance of Toydarian lakes.

Mouthpiece

Webbed feet

WATTO'S SHISHA

SCENTER

DATA FILE

◆ When he first settled on Tatooine, Watto hung out with Jawas, picking up stories and legends of great scrap finds in the desert—as well as crafty ways to sell faulty pit droids.

◆ A firm but fair master, Watto treats his slaves more decently than most.

LOSING
Boasting to friends of his colossal bets, Watto sets himself up for a disastrous loss when his favorite Podracer, Sebulba, loses the Boonta Eve event. What really infuriates Watto is the thought of the astronomical sums he could have won if he had bet on the winner, his own slave, Anakin Skywalker.

Sebulba

AMONG THE PODRACER PILOTS of the rugged Outer Rim circuit, Sebulba has accelerated his way to the top with an unbeatable combination of courage, skill, and outrageous cheating. His murderous tactics often bring his competitors down in flames, but he knows where the race cameras are placed and manages to avoid being seen. In spite of his crimes, Sebulba has found that in Mos Espa success makes its own rules. Now enjoying the power and prestige of being a top racer, the unscrupulous Dug has just one thorn in his side—the young Podracer named Anakin Skywalker.

Sebulba's anger towards Anakin stems chiefly from fear. If the young human were ever to win a race, even by accident, Sebulba would be disgraced. The hateful Dug intends to make sure this never happens.

Sebulba is an arboreal Dug from Malastare. Swinging from tree to tree on this high-gravity planet has made Dugs strong and well coordinated. Most have no desire to leave Malastare—and this is fine with the rest of the galaxy since Dugs are notorious bullies.

Split-X radiators

Concealed flame emitter weapon

Combustion chambers

Boost afterburner

Massive engine nozzles

Control cables

Repulsor "threader" helps Podracer avoid obstacles

Control Pod

Compressor

Stabilizing vane

Sebulba's race graphics

Sebulba's Podracer

Sebulba's giant Collor Pondrat Plug-F Mammoth Split-X Podracer would be classified as illegally large if race officials were ever able to take a close enough look at it. Concealed weapons like Sebulba's flame emitter lend that special winning edge during a race.

Podracer cockpits are customized to suit the particular driver's anatomy. Sebulba's complex array of control pedals and levers is woven into an even more complicated automatic data transmission bank that provides readouts of all engine conditions during the race.

The race crowds love a winner, and Sebulba delivers victories time and again. The odious Dug plays to the crowd when in their sight, and has become the heavy favorite in the betting pits.

Main combustion pyrometer readout

Pre-feed pyrometer readout

Throttle lever

Aeration mix gauge

Second-stage fuel flow rate indicator

Crowd-pleasing grin

Wattle

Sebulba, Podrace Anarchist

Sebulba is highly skilled Podracer, but he was not quite good enough to make it to the top on ability alone. When he found that intimidation and race violations were quite effective in gaining victory, he refined these abilities and began to add secret weapons to his racing machine. Dispatching opponents without getting caught is now the chief sporting aspect of Podracing for the malevolent Dug.

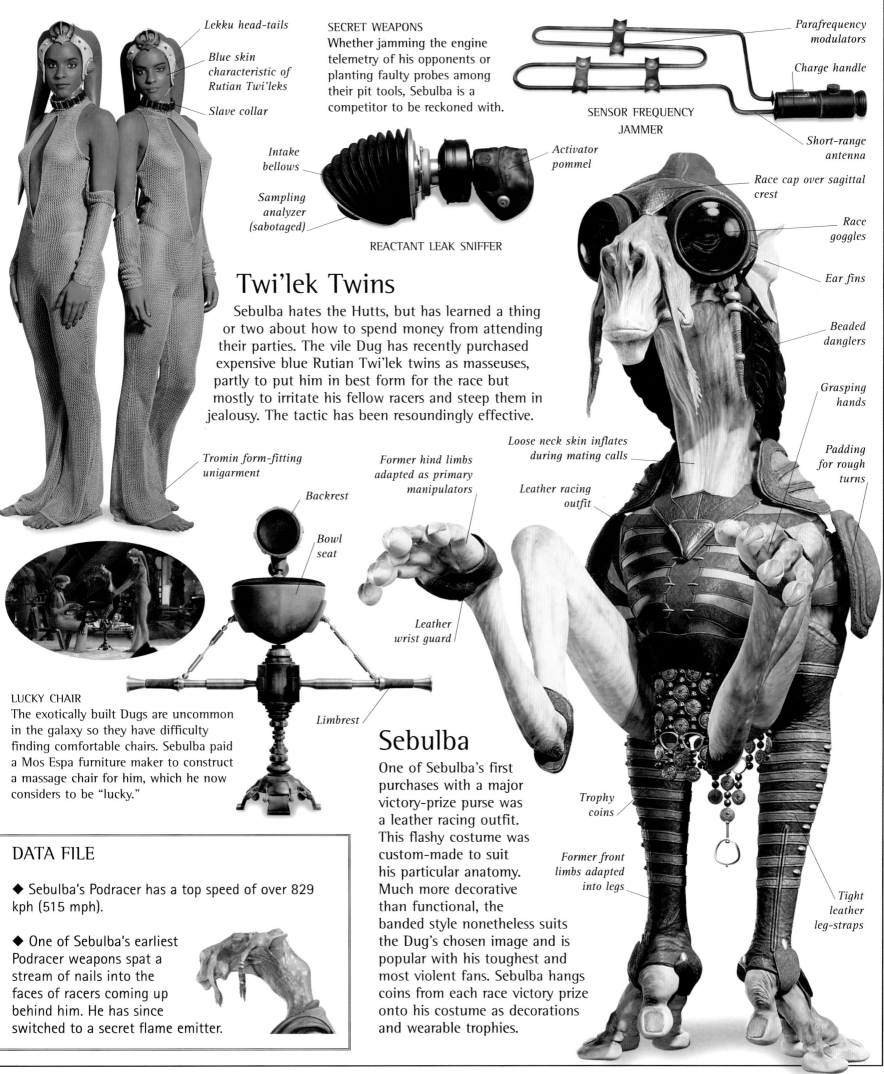

Lekku head-tails

Blue skin characteristic of Rutian Twi'leks

Slave collar

SECRET WEAPONS
Whether jamming the engine telemetry of his opponents or planting faulty probes among their pit tools, Sebulba is a competitor to be reckoned with.

Parafrequency modulators

Charge handle

SENSOR FREQUENCY JAMMER

Short-range antenna

Intake bellows

Activator pommel

Sampling analyzer (sabotaged)

REACTANT LEAK SNIFFER

Race cap over sagittal crest

Race goggles

Ear fins

Beaded danglers

Twi'lek Twins

Sebulba hates the Hutts, but has learned a thing or two about how to spend money from attending their parties. The vile Dug has recently purchased expensive blue Rutian Twi'lek twins as masseuses, partly to put him in best form for the race but mostly to irritate his fellow racers and steep them in jealousy. The tactic has been resoundingly effective.

Grasping hands

Padding for rough turns

Tromin form-fitting unigarment

Former hind limbs adapted as primary manipulators

Loose neck skin inflates during mating calls

Leather racing outfit

Backrest

Bowl seat

Leather wrist guard

Limbrest

LUCKY CHAIR
The exotically built Dugs are uncommon in the galaxy so they have difficulty finding comfortable chairs. Sebulba paid a Mos Espa furniture maker to construct a massage chair for him, which he now considers to be "lucky."

Sebulba

One of Sebulba's first purchases with a major victory-prize purse was a leather racing outfit. This flashy costume was custom-made to suit his particular anatomy. Much more decorative than functional, the banded style nonetheless suits the Dug's chosen image and is popular with his toughest and most violent fans. Sebulba hangs coins from each race victory prize onto his costume as decorations and wearable trophies.

Trophy coins

Former front limbs adapted into legs

Tight leather leg-straps

DATA FILE

◆ Sebulba's Podracer has a top speed of over 829 kph (515 mph).

◆ One of Sebulba's earliest Podracer weapons spat a stream of nails into the faces of racers coming up behind him. He has since switched to a secret flame emitter.

Podrace Crews

PODRACERS are complex machines that require extensive maintenance and frequent repair. The mechanical stress of running high-performance engines at up to 800 kilometers per hour takes a heavy toll on any Tatooine Podracer. The pit crews rebuild the battered machines and prepare them for the next big race. Assisted by frantic pit droids and pestered by race officials citing violations, Podracer crews must also put up with the egos of the racers themselves. In spite of it all, the crews take great satisfaction in knowing that they make all the action possible.

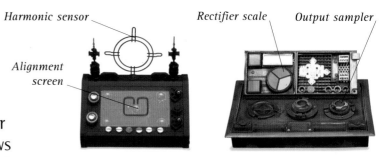

Harmonic sensor

Rectifier scale *Output sampler*

Alignment screen

POWER OUTPUT ANALYZER   INSTRUMENT CALIBRATOR

Podracing crews use specialized instruments to analyze engine performance and diagnose faults. Tools should be standardized for safety and fairness, but in practice no two crews have the same gear.

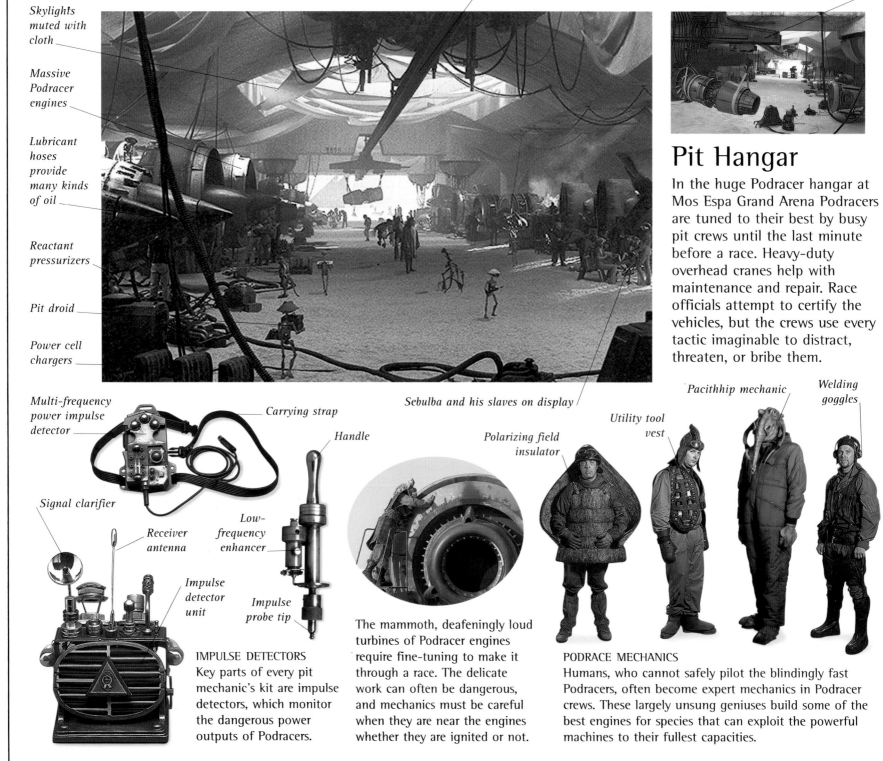

Skylights muted with cloth

Massive Podracer engines

Lubricant hoses provide many kinds of oil

Reactant pressurizers

Pit droid

Power cell chargers

Overhead crane track

Heavy cranes move Podracer engines

Pit Hangar

In the huge Podracer hangar at Mos Espa Grand Arena Podracers are tuned to their best by busy pit crews until the last minute before a race. Heavy-duty overhead cranes help with maintenance and repair. Race officials attempt to certify the vehicles, but the crews use every tactic imaginable to distract, threaten, or bribe them.

Multi-frequency power impulse detector

Carrying strap

Sebulba and his slaves on display

Pacithhip mechanic

Welding goggles

Utility tool vest

Handle

Polarizing field insulator

Signal clarifier

Receiver antenna

Low-frequency enhancer

Impulse detector unit

Impulse probe tip

IMPULSE DETECTORS
Key parts of every pit mechanic's kit are impulse detectors, which monitor the dangerous power outputs of Podracers.

The mammoth, deafeningly loud turbines of Podracer engines require fine-tuning to make it through a race. The delicate work can often be dangerous, and mechanics must be careful when they are near the engines whether they are ignited or not.

PODRACE MECHANICS
Humans, who cannot safely pilot the blindingly fast Podracers, often become expert mechanics in Podracer crews. These largely unsung geniuses build some of the best engines for species that can exploit the powerful machines to their fullest capacities.

Pit droids are such a common sight near Podracers that they go mostly unnoticed, in spite of the bizarre antics they sometimes engage in when trying to get a job done. The real mechanics are left to make the complex decisions and oversee customized engine modifications.

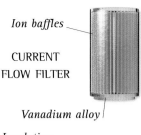

Ion baffles

CURRENT
FLOW FILTER

Vanadium alloy

Insulating sleeve   *Firing terminal*

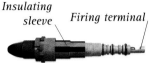

PODRACER POWER PLUG

DATA FILE

◆ The fatality rate in the frontier-world Boonta Eve Classic is higher than in any other Podrace in the Outer Rim.

◆ A tap on the "nose" of a pit droid causes it to deactivate and collapse into a compressed form for easy storage (and to keep it out of trouble).

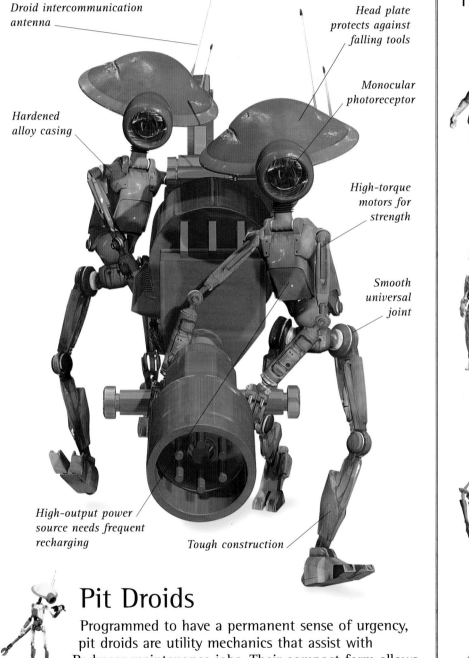

Droid intercommunication antenna

Head plate protects against falling tools

Hardened alloy casing

Monocular photoreceptor

High-torque motors for strength

Smooth universal joint

High-output power source needs frequent recharging

Tough construction

Pit Droids

Programmed to have a permanent sense of urgency, pit droids are utility mechanics that assist with Podracer maintenance jobs. Their compact form allows them to reach small parts and linkages in and under the big engines. Pit droids are built with minimal logic processors so they take orders without asking personal or superfluous questions. However, this also leaves them easily confused and apt to get into trouble when left to their own devices.

THE MAIN PODRACER CONTENDERS

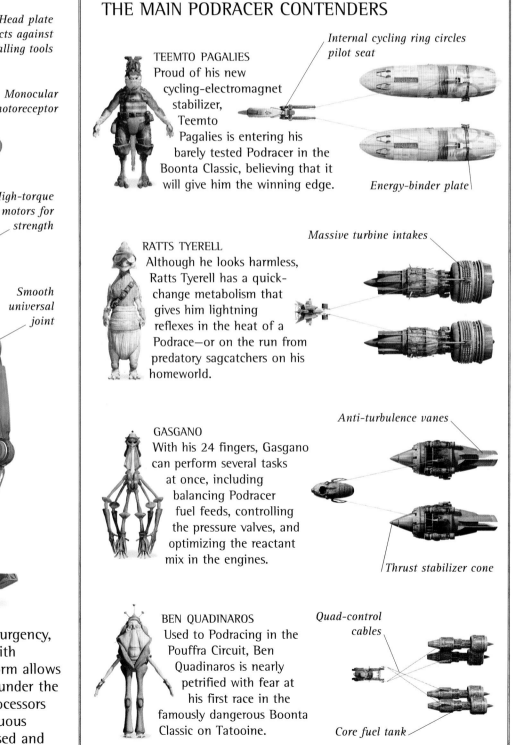

Internal cycling ring circles pilot seat

TEEMTO PAGALIES
Proud of his new cycling-electromagnet stabilizer, Teemto Pagalies is entering his barely tested Podracer in the Boonta Classic, believing that it will give him the winning edge.

Energy-binder plate

Massive turbine intakes

RATTS TYERELL
Although he looks harmless, Ratts Tyerell has a quick-change metabolism that gives him lightning reflexes in the heat of a Podrace—or on the run from predatory sagcatchers on his homeworld.

Anti-turbulence vanes

GASGANO
With his 24 fingers, Gasgano can perform several tasks at once, including balancing Podracer fuel feeds, controlling the pressure valves, and optimizing the reactant mix in the engines.

Thrust stabilizer cone

Quad-control cables

BEN QUADINAROS
Used to Podracing in the Pouffra Circuit, Ben Quadinaros is nearly petrified with fear at his first race in the famously dangerous Boonta Classic on Tatooine.

Core fuel tank

The Podrace Crowd

NOTHING COMPARES to the sheer spectacle of Podracing as witnessed in the worlds of the Outer Rim. Racers tear through rugged landscapes driving all manner of non-standardized machines in a contest of raw nerve and razor-edge calculation. Each racer has fought blistering competition to get on the circuit, rules are seen as guidelines, and safety concerns are thrown to the wind. To witness an all-star event like the Boonta Eve Podrace on Tatooine is to live the thrill of racing at its most intense.

Race course through desert wilderness — Pit hangar — North stands — Starters' box and finish line

Arena citadel with betting floors

Concessions concourse

Starting grid

Shuttle terminal

West stands

Patches repair damage from being shot down

Jawa-built envelope

Cheap channel race omnicam

Mos Espa Arena

The atmosphere before a Podrace is electric. Spectators take their seats in the stands; the rich enter their boxes or elevating platforms for an aerial view; Podracers are prepared in the pit building and the betting floors are scenes of feverish activity as the odds are updated every few seconds.

Parade of racers' flags

The system for determining the starting lineup of the Boonta Eve race involves an apparently baffling combination of performance statistics, outright bribery, and random chance.

SIDE VIEW

Transmission antenna

The starters' box holds race officials, the starting light, and three lap indicators.

Starting light — Lap indicators

Repulsorlift wing

Multiple lenses catch a range of angles on key turns and speed flats

FLOONORP

SABRIQUET

DRIXFAR

Race cameras used to be built into the rocks along the course to help spectators catch every thrill, but these were all stolen or shot to pieces. Now, a fleet of hovering cam droids is used.

PODRACE CAM DROID

MUSICAL INSTRUMENTS
Musicians stroll the stands on race day, entertaining the crowds for contributions. Many of the improvised instruments they play are made from engine parts.

FANATICAL SPECTATORS
Thousands of race fans fill the vast capacity of Mos Espa Grand Arena for the big races such as the Boonta Eve. Every language in the galaxy is heard from the Podrace enthusiasts as entire fortunes are wagered on current favorites and hopeless longshots.

DATA FILE

◆ Mos Espa Arena holds more than 100,000 spectators.

◆ Race contestants are granted seating for chosen supporters. Anakin's mother and friends watch the race from an elevating platform.

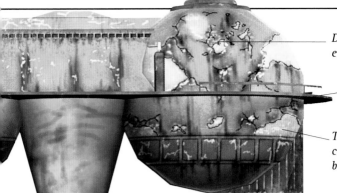

Double ballonets inside envelope for stability

Supporting framework

Tibanna gas compound keeps balloon afloat

Podrace Balloons

The Hutts charge fans to use viewscreen channels supplied by official repulsorlift race cameras. However, a gray market of cheap channels fed by balloon cameras has sprung up, since only permanent and repulsorlift-powered cameras are controlled. Some brave spectators even watch the race from rented balloons, which are often shot down by drunk and disorderly fans or angry losing betters.

High tensile-strength cables

Channel select

Display mode select

Spectator gondola

Grip bars

Motion-tracking scanner

Stereo-view double eyepieces

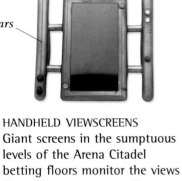

RACE ELECTROBINOCULARS

HANDHELD VIEWSCREENS
Giant screens in the sumptuous levels of the Arena Citadel betting floors monitor the views from the race cameras. However, most fans prefer to to watch the race in the stands using rented screens or electrobinoculars.

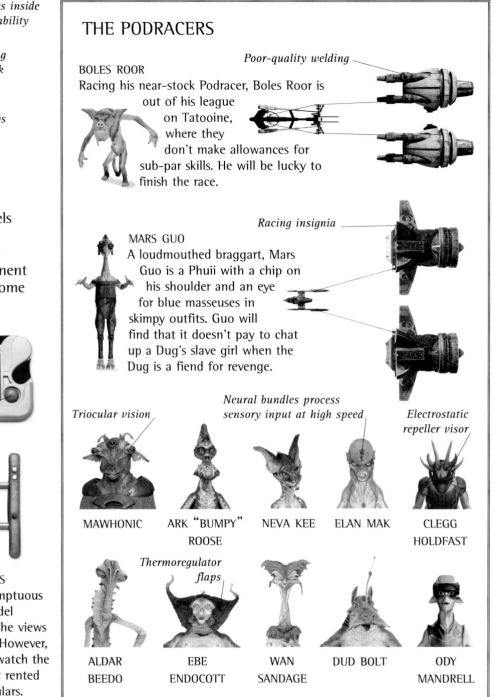

THE PODRACERS

BOLES ROOR
Racing his near-stock Podracer, Boles Roor is out of his league on Tatooine, where they don't make allowances for sub-par skills. He will be lucky to finish the race.

Poor-quality welding

MARS GUO
A loudmouthed braggart, Mars Guo is a Phuii with a chip on his shoulder and an eye for blue masseuses in skimpy outfits. Guo will find that it doesn't pay to chat up a Dug's slave girl when the Dug is a fiend for revenge.

Racing insignia

Triocular vision

Neural bundles process sensory input at high speed

Electrostatic repeller visor

MAWHONIC

ARK "BUMPY" ROOSE

NEVA KEE

ELAN MAK

CLEGG HOLDFAST

Thermoregulator flaps

ALDAR BEEDO

EBE ENDOCOTT

WAN SANDAGE

DUD BOLT

ODY MANDRELL

Jabba the Hutt

Somewhere in Mos Espa there is a little-known official who legally rules the city, but the wealthy gangster "First Citizen" Jabba the Hutt is really in control. Jabba presides over the Boonta Eve race from the best box seats in the arena, thinking only of the profits he will reap through his gambling organizations. His major-domo Bib Fortuna attends to every arrangement, keeping Jabba's entertainment running as smoothly as his criminal operations.

Jabba the Hutt

Bib Fortuna, Jabba's Twi'lek major-domo

Diva Shaliqua, one of Jabba's slaves

Jabba's shisha

Chokk, an armed bodyguard

R5-X2 computes betting odds and Jabba's winnings

Huttese glyphs of good fortune

Diva Funquita, Gardulla's assistant

Gardulla the Hutt, Jabba's guest and sometime rival

Dwarf nunas brought back by one of Jabba's assassins from a recent mission

Tatooine Inhabitants

A FRONTIER WORLD, the desert planet Tatooine lies on an important hyperspace route between the civilized planets of the galactic core and the distant star systems of the Outer Rim. Traders and smugglers run all manner of goods through Tatooine's spaceports, answering to few authorities besides the gangster Hutts. On the desert surface, inhabitants include desperate settlers, impoverished spacers, aliens of dubious reputation, droids of all kinds, along with the scattered representatives of Tatooine's native populations, who are best adapted to life on this difficult world.

Spacers willing to run routes into the risky areas beyond Tatooine wait for work in a streetside café, where cooled table slabs offer some respite from the heat. Games like triga help to pass the time.

Drann player markers *Sett player home*

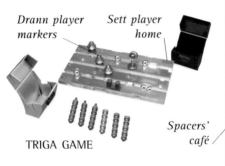

TRIGA GAME

Spacers' café

Cheap imitation chiller tables offer no coolth

Marketplace

In the crowded marketplace alleys of Mos Espa, various quarters specialize in particular types of trade. Some serve the day-to-day needs of local inhabitants, while others house droid mechanics, engine repairers, and—if you know where to look—illegal weapons dealers.

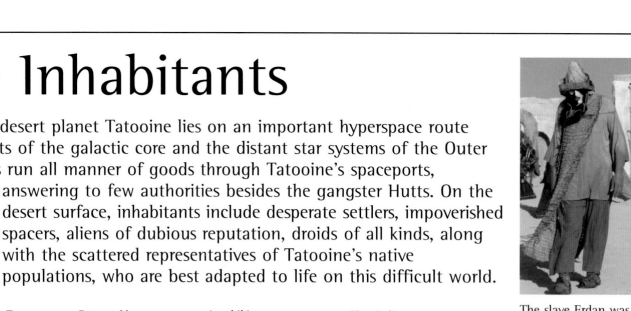

Teguar deal-maker *Retractable awning* *Amphibious gorgs cooked at street stalls* *Non-indigenous species recovered from freighter bilge*

Locals keep a low profile

Broken antenna

Gorg dipping sauces *R2-D2*

Welding droid

The slave Erdan was chemically enlarged by his owner to increase his work-rate. His face was patterned as a mark of ownership.

GORGMONGER
Gragra claims to keep her amphibian food stock in a large basement culture pool, but she actually grows them in a sewer zone under Mos Espa.

Intensity controls

Compressor

Coolth emitter vents

COOLING UNIT
Many street vendors in Mos Espa keep cooling units near their wares to draw potential customers from the hot streets.

Head salvaged from Temirca droid

Montoro serving drone body

Repair worker arms

Podracer engine shroud

Droids

In the Outer Rim, ancient and heavily repaired droids can often be seen lurching through back alleys. Also common are exotic hybrids made of parts combined from dissimilar droids. The resulting machines tend to have either limited mentalities or personalities as bizarre as their origins.

Ignored or derided by the gangster and spacer classes, Mos Espa settlers try their hardest to avoid involvement in local disputes or gunfights.

Beasts of Burden

Tatooine's heat, dust, and sandstorms can damage mechanical transport, but animals make ideal beasts of burden. Dewbacks are used all over Tatooine, eopies are common only around Mos Espa, and banthas are the exclusive mounts of the Sandpeople.

Suspicious-looking luggage

White skin pigmentation reflects sunlight

Scaly skin retains moisture

DEWBACK

Flexible snout for uncovering sand lichen that grow just beneath the planet surface

Broad feet for sand travel

EOPIE

Natives of Tatooine, eopies are able to carry heavy loads in intense heat without tiring.

Long barrel for accuracy

Gaffi stick

Sandproof bindings

Stolen projectile rifle

Protective eye lenses

Filtering sandmask

Bound hands

Heavy cloak and bindings protect against sand and sun

Indigenous to Tatooine, Jawas have become used to contact with space travelers. Many Jawas act as metal scavengers and equipment-repair craftworkers.

Ammo bandoleer

Clan-crafted leatherwork

At times, sandpeople steal guns but strongly favor traditional club and ax weapons for close quarters combat.

Sling

Power cell

Long robe allows free movement and ventilation

Sandpeople take pot shots at fast-moving Podracers from remote sections of the Podrace course, hoping to strand and attack race pilots.

BACKPACK COOLERS
Twin suns make for searing hot middays, so pedestrians in Mos Espa often wear personal cooling units.

DATA FILE

◆ Jawa clans can be distinguished by subtle differences in their cloak designs.

◆ Children in Mos Espa play with fortune-telling "Eyes of Mesra," an old desert tradition.

Sandpeople

Unlike the Jawas, the native Tatooine Sandpeople have not adapted to easy contact with outworld settlers. Resentful of incursions in their territory, Sandpeople prey upon travelers and are known as Tusken Raiders. Renowned for their savagery, Tusken Raiders are lethally dangerous and not to be trifled with.

Handle

Ion charger exhaust

Collector

Intake

SANDSTAT
Sand and dust blows into every corner of Mos Espa; the fastidious clean up with electrostatic sandstats.

Bandaged feet

Chancellor Valorum

A LIFETIME OF PREPARATION led to Finis Valorum's election as Supreme Chancellor of the Galactic Senate. Valorum inherited the legacy of a family whose greatest members had each represented more than 1,000 worlds. Centuries ago, a Valorum served as Supreme Chancellor. Finis Valorum has now equalled this achievement, ruling the entire Republic from the galactic seat on Coruscant. However, he has also inherited a government grown weak from its own success: the galactic representatives have become distanced from their people and now the entire system is degenerating.

Distinguished gray hair

Premature aging from pressures of governing

Veda cloth robe

Ornate overcloak

Blue band symbolic of Supreme Chancellor

Coruscant

The galactic capital, Coruscant, is almost entirely covered with skyscrapers. These kilometers-high buildings provide living space for more than a trillion inhabitants, including the thousands of representatives in the Senate Chamber. The planet is entirely dependent on outside support to survive, consuming resource shipments from a steady stream of vast freighters.

Sei Taria

Chancellor Valorum's administrative aide, Sei Taria assists him in confirming the fine details of necessary procedural regulations. She has learned much from Senator Palpatine.

Septsilk robe signifies wealth

Blue skin screens out harmful radiation

Chagrian horns used for intimidating display

Lethorns

DATA FILE

◆ Coruscant has been the center of galactic government for tens of thousands of years. Its early history is shrouded in legend.

◆ Increasingly, Supreme Chancellor Valorum has been influenced by senators such as Palpatine to compromise what he knows is right for the sake of approved procedure.

Mas Amedda

The stern Chagrian Mas Amedda is responsible for keeping order in the Senate. Accused of misusing his parliamentary powers for bribes, Amedda stands firm to his own code of honor.

AIR TAXIS

Multi-spectrum headlights *Communications antenna*

Air taxis carry passengers throughout the bewildering maze of canyons and pinnacles in Coruscant's skyscraper landscape.

High altitude repulsors

Platform seating *Senate guard*

Repulsorlift

SENATE PLATFORMS

The vast amphitheater of the Senate Rotunda is lined with 1,024 platforms. The majority are used by sectorial senators, who represent their own planet and hundreds of others in a galactic sector. The remaining platforms are available for limited periods to alliances, commercial powers, or individual planets with special causes to bring before the senate.

When a senate representative is recognized for official speech, their senate platform detaches itself from the rotunda and flies out into the open chamber for prominence.

Rodian representative on senate platform

Senate Guard

The guards of the Galactic Senate wear striking robes of blue, symbolizing the Senate's supreme authority and the long tradition of its wise and just rule. The large crest and simple drape are ceremonial effects rather than functional designs.

Highly visible crest

Muzzle brake dampens rifle blast

Large, unwieldy ceremonial rifle

HOVERCAM SIDE VIEW

Control antenna

Hovercam

Wide angle lens *Telephoto lens*

A squadron of flying hovercams patrols the Rotunda to record the speeches and votes of the Senate representatives. Some hovercam operators abuse their responsibility and omit to record certain individuals, while others allow unscrupulous senators to alter the record of their words after they are spoken.

Repulsor floaters

THE DIVERSITY OF THE SENATE

A vast range of alien species populates the Senate Rotunda, hailing from every corner of the Republic. Among them can be seen the traditional costumes of hundreds of planets, as well as many fashions particular to Coruscant.

Dual mouths for stereo language

Brain in neck hump

Alderaan aides

LIANA MERIAN

AGRIPPA ALDRETE

TENDAU BENDON

SENATOR YARUA FROM KASHYYYK

Renowned for their tempers, Wookiee senators are nonetheless possessed of a firm sense of fair justice. Senator Yarua finds commercial power within the senate reprehensible and is determined to restore justice to galactic government.

Blue color hints at Palpatine's interest in the Chancellorship

Elaborate cloak asserts sectorial authority

Senator Palpatine

ENDLESS PATIENCE has been Palpatine's key to success. Passed over as a young politician and repeatedly turned down for office and appointment, he has learned the value of quiet persistence. Palpatine has risen through the ranks to attain the powerful office of sectorial representative to the Galactic Senate on Coruscant. Palpatine represents some 36 worlds in a backwater sector, of which his provincial home planet of Naboo is typical. Turning this background to his advantage, Palpatine has been ever-present in the halls of galactic politics, impressing friend and opponent alike with his unassuming demeanor and simple but powerful insights into how the galaxy could be better run.

Over time Palpatine has developed a reputation as someone apart from intrigue and corruption, as he patiently condemns the many abuses of bureaucracy that come to his attention. It is little surprise to insiders that he is nominated for the office of Supreme Chancellor.

Palpatine's apartment is modest compared to the stunning palaces of other sectorial representatives

PALPATINE'S APARTMENT Few outsiders are welcomed into Palpatine's scarlet chambers. They are the exclusive haunt of his trusted confidants until Amidala arrives on Coruscant to plead her case.

Naboo-style bloused sleeves with long cuffs

Royal handmaiden

Queen Amidala

Strange red decor

Diplomat

Palpatine never favored Naboo's previous sovereign, King Veruna, even after the stubborn ruler heeded Palpatine's suggestions to become more involved in foreign affairs. Queen Amidala suits Palpatine, since he believes she will better follow his directions.

Before they meet at the Senate, Queen Amidala has only seen Palpatine in person once, at her coronation. She half-suspects that his concern for Naboo is secondary to his political ambitions.

DATA FILE

◆ Senator Palapatine's unusual choice of art objects reveals to Queen Amidala that he has left his Naboo heritage far behind and has adopted a more worldly point of view.

ROUTE TO SUCCESS Palpatine consistently favors less concern for senatorial legality and procedure and more attention to simply doing what he considers needs to be done. It is as

a result of this practical attitude that many look forward to the clear-minded leadership that Palpatine promises to provide.

The Senate

THE POWER of sectorial senators is immense, as they control access to the Senate for hundreds of planets. The temptations that go with such power are equally great. Corrupt senators are no longer unusual, even at the highest level, and few Republic citizens expect anything but empty promises and word games from anyone who sets foot on Coruscant. In truth, many senators are simply lazy and greedy, but by doing nothing to stop the spread of evil they become some of its greatest supporters.

Gesture showing objection

MOT NOT RAB

Gesture denying guilt

BASKOL YEESRIM

Gesture blaming others

PASSEL ARGENTE

Gesture of reassurance

HOROX RYYDER

Consorts

Senators are attended by assistants, aides, and consorts according to customs and traditions of their home planets and sectors. Many young aides are repulsed by the abuses of government they see on Coruscant, but they stay on, reluctant to lose their positions of power.

Rare red-skinned Lethan Twi'lek

Lekku (head-tail)

Ear flaps store fat

Over-indulgent features

Gaudy robe

SENATORIAL POLITICS

Many senators have become known for judicious nonalignment, allowing their worlds to profit from supplying both sides in conflicts. Critics comment that three-eyed Malastarians like Baskol Yeesrim can not only see both sides of an issue, but can always spot their position of advantage right in the center.

Senator Toonbuck Toora's last traces of idealism have been eradicated by watching the downfall of the just and from counting the profits that flow from finding loopholes in the law. She now counts as friends criminal senators she once held in contempt and rewards loyal supporters with well-paid appointments as consorts or aides.

CONSORT TO TOONBUCK TOORA

Senator Orn Free Taa

Indulgent lifestyles are nowhere more extreme than on Coruscant. Senator Orn Free Taa has found possibilities beyond his wildest dreams. He views galactic government as merely the sport of the mighty like himself. In his excesses he has grown vile and corpulent, but he is confident that money and power will always make him attractive.

DATA FILE

◆ Lavender was chosen for the color of the Senate interior because it was the only hue that had never been associated with war, anger, or mourning in any culture in the Republic.

◆ Senator Tikkes moved from business to Coruscant politics to make some *real* money.

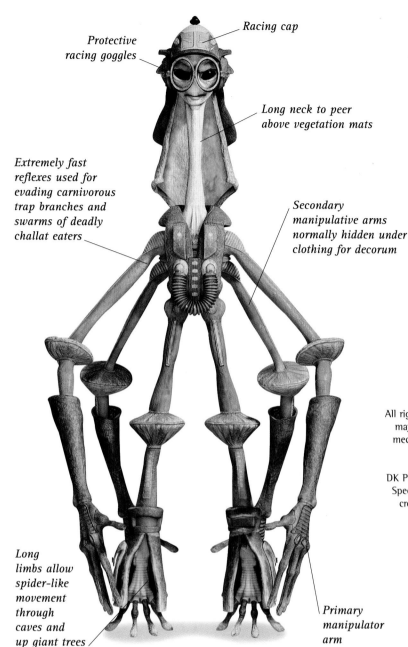

Racing cap

Protective
racing goggles

Long neck to peer
above vegetation mats

Extremely fast
reflexes used for
evading carnivorous
trap branches and
swarms of deadly
challat eaters

Secondary
manipulative arms
normally hidden under
clothing for decorum

Long
limbs allow
spider-like
movement
through
caves and
up giant trees

Primary
manipulator
arm

GASGANO

A DK PUBLISHING BOOK

PROJECT ART EDITORS Iain Morris & Jane Thomas
PROJECT EDITOR Simon Beecroft
US EDITOR Sarah Hines Stephens
MANAGING ART EDITOR Cathy Tincknell
MANAGING EDITOR Joanna Devereux
DESIGNERS Kim Browne & Guy Harvey
DTP DESIGNER Jill Bunyan
PRODUCTION Steve Lang
US PICTURE RESEARCH Cara Evangelista
US PHOTO LIBRARY Tina Mills
ILM IMAGE COORDINATOR Christine Owens

First American Edition, 1999
2 4 6 8 10 9 7 5 3 1
Published in the United States by
DK Publishing, Inc., 95 Madison Avenue, New York, New York 10016

DK Publishing books are available at special discounts for bulk purchases for sales promotions or premiums. Special editions, including personalized covers, excerpts of existing guides, and corporate imprints can be created in large quantities for specific needs. For more information, contact Special Markets Dept./DK Publishing, Inc./95 Madison Ave./New York, NY 10016/Fax: 800-600-9098.

Library of Congress Cataloguing-in-Publication Data
Reynolds, David West.
    Star Wars, episode 1 : visual dictionary / written by David West Reynolds. — 1st American ed.
        p.   cm.
    SUMMARY: Text and illustrations present characters from episode 1 of "Star Wars" and the technology they use, including Qui-Gon Jinn and his wrist hologram projector, the space freighters of the Neimoidians, and the lightsabers of the Jedi Knights.
    ISBN 0-7894-4701-0
    1. Star Wars, episode 1, the phantom menace (Motion picture)—Miscellanea. (1. Star Wars, episode 1, the phantom menace (Motion picture)) I. Title
PN1997.S6595 R49 1999
791.43'72—dc21   98-18082
                                                   CIP
Colour reproduction by Colourscan, Singapore
Printed in the U.S.A. by RR Donnelley & Sons Company

Acknowledgements

Many hands made this book possible, and the Captain would like to express special thanks to a few in particular:
Ty Teiger and his prop department at Leavesden Studios fabricated the amazing range of marvelous guns and gadgets filling these pages to overflowing; the book is also a parade of the sumptuous and extraordinary costumes created by costume designer Trisha Biggar and her team; special additional fabrication was provided by ILM modelmaker Don Bies, who cracked open the battle droid head for us; Ed Maggiani and Steve Cymszo made sure that even the most diminutive Jedi Master had a custom-made lightsaber; design consultant Iain Morris somehow managed to be multiple persons at once, and one or two of him helmed the outstanding layouts herein that would even make text copied from a phone book look brilliant; art editor Jane Thomas joined us at Skywalker Ranch to provide vital help, making possible the completion of the book design in a fortnight or so (give or take); David Pickering's sage editorial influence still hovered over my keyboard like the spirit of Obi-Wan; but when I was prepared to keenly regret his absence, DK editor Simon Beecroft appeared courageously to offer (along with lots of editorial work) crucial good cheer, stimulating conversation, and the editorial encouragement that makes really satisfying work possible; Lucasfilm editor Sarah Hines Stephens also stepped in for this book

with a smile and a keen eye, keeping the evolving backstories in harmony with the rest of the Star Wars universe; charming Lucas Licensing Publishing Coordinator Cara Evangelista provided great stacks of reference material to the team from the beginning, when there was chaos and the darkness was without form; all this imagery was forged at the anvils of Image Coordinator Tina Mills, who must have a separate universe in her office and a large staff of invisible extra assistants to accomplish all that she and her staff do; FBI Special Agent R. Matthew Bliss offered the benefit of his expertise in refining the secret profile of Darth Maul, marking what was probably the first time a U.S. federal agent has professionally explored the background of a Sith Lord; chief engineer George Stephens Whitcomb, formerly of the U.S. Navy nuclear aircraft carrier CV-66 U.S.S. America, was, as always, an inspiration in speculative functionality; poet, thief, and swordsman extraordinaire Jack "Tony" Bobo, Esq., provided immeasurable assistance in firing my imagination, as did treasure hunter and writer Carl "Ray the Barbarian" Cart, whose fiction is concentrated like nitroglycerine and who sets the high standard toward which I strive; Prof. Gregory S. Aldrete, Ph.D., of the History department at the University of Wisconsin at Green Bay, offered ongoing conversations on the links between society, art, artifacts, and culture, which influence my entire

approach to interpretative analysis, even in the Star Wars universe; Hugh Quarshie contributed one of the most interesting discussions I enjoyed during all my time on the film sets at Leavesden, including his privileged insight into the intrigue within the Naboo royalty; Neal Porter and Fiona Macmillan at DK were a pleasure to work with and kept me proud of the team I was on; Lucasfilm editor Jane Mason helped the book take shape in its earliest stages; Lucasfilm Director of Publishing Lucy Wilson stuck with me and my unusual circumstances for another rewarding project; and finally, Ann Marie Reynolds offered me support throughout and proved the value of her editorial influence on yet another project, making sure that Simon didn't see anything that was really first draft.

DK Publishing would also like to thank:
Alex Ivanov and David Owens for additional photography; Justin Graham, Scott Carter, Matthew Azeveda, Paloma Añoveros, Susan Copley, Danielle Roode, and Fay David for additional research; David John for additional editorial work; John Kelly and Mark Regardsoe for additional design work.